When I Hid My Caste

Stories

Baburao Bagul

Translated by JERRY PINTO

SPEAKING
TIGER

SPEAKING TIGER PUBLISHING PVT. LTD
4381/4, Ansari Road, Daryaganj
New Delhi 110002

Originally published as *Jevha Mi Jaat Chorli Hoti* in
Marathi by Akshar Prakashan in 1963

Published in English by Speaking Tiger in hardback 2018

ISBN: 978-93-86702-95-1
eISBN: 978-93-86702-93-7

10 9 8 7 6 5 4 3 2 1

Typeset in Adobe Garamond Pro by SÜRYA, New Delhi
Printed at Sanat Printers, Kundli

Contents

Introduction   *vii*

Prisoner of Darkness   1

Bohada   19

Streetwalker   33

Gangster   44

Dassehra Sacrifice   51

Monkey   62

Competition   71

Revolt   90

Pesuk   104

When I Hid My Caste   116

Translator's Acknowledgements   137

Introduction

BABURAO RAMJI BAGUL was born on 17 July 1931 in Vihitgaon, Nashik Disrict, Maharashtra, in a desperately poor Dalit family. At ten years old, he was sent to live with his maternal aunt in Mumbai. He went to the local municipal school from where he matriculated. After that there was no education for him. He did odd jobs to pull his weight in the family until he found a permanent job in the railways.

Bagul's aunt lived in the Matunga Labour Camp, a complex constructed by the Bombay Municipal Corporation for Dalit labour from the hinterland. The buildings were dingy, the land marshy and infested with mosquitoes. Large families lived in cramped single rooms with little or no ventilation. What space there was between buildings was overrun by hens, stray dogs, cats and naked children. There was no sanitation to speak of. Friends from the outside world who visited Bagul were revolted by the all-pervading stench that hung in the air. It was a wonder that people could exist here. It was an even greater wonder that Bagul wrote in these surroundings. But then there were two great fires blazing in those dark, dank, squalid environs, putting spunk and spirit into the young residents of the camp—Dr B.R. Ambedkar's Scheduled Caste Federation office and the Communist Party's study circles. Together they kept the camp buzzing with intellectual activity.

Bagul drew his strength from both. Marx gave the worker in him an idea of his worth. Ambedkar showed him, as a Dalit, who his enemy was. Their double influence is evident in the title story of the present collection, vividly translated by Jerry Pinto. The protagonist of 'When I Hid My Caste' arrives in the town where his employer, the railways, has posted him. A bunch of workers asks him his caste. 'I roared like a thunderclap on hearing this: "Why do you ask me my caste? Can you not see who I am? Me, I am a Mumbaikar. I fight the good fight. I give my life in the defence of the right. I have freed India from bondage and I am now her strength."' At the end of the story, when he is lynched by his erstwhile mates, he says, 'When was I beaten by them? It was Manu who thrashed me.'

Shankarrao Kharat and Annabhau Sathe, the other big names in early Dalit fiction, were ten years older than Bagul. Some of their work had made a deep impact on readers. But it was nothing as compared to the veritable storm that Bagul's *Jevha Mi Jaat Chorli Hoti* created when it appeared in 1963. He knocked readers off their feet by the sheer elemental force of his stories. But, more importantly, he liberated younger Dalit writers from the shackles of literary Marathi. They were now free to write in their own tongues. If readers, weaned on the preponderantly romantic literature of upper-caste Marathi writers, found these new voices difficult to stomach, so be it.

Ambedkar had called upon Dalits to educate, agitate and organize. The three imperatives that drove Dalit literature were vidroha (revolt), vedana (pain) and nakar (dissent). In Bagul's most painful, stomach-churning story, 'Vidroha' ('The Revolt'), the protagonist revolts against doing the caste-enforced work of lifting human excreta. 'Pesuk' registers the inhuman pain Savitri has suffered at the hands of her husband. In 'Bohada', the protagonist Damu stands up to the village powers, the very incarnation of dissent. Years later, continuing the tradition, Namdeo Dhasal was to demand 'Which donkey was given the name Independence? / Which room in Ramrajya did you occupy?' Even more iconoclastically, Tryambak Sapkale rejected God outright in a deliberately hybrid mix of Marathi and English: 'We godmakers / Serve notice on you / For negligence of duty. / Your services are not required.'

Bagul's stories enforce this foundation of revolt, pain and dissent with verbs that act like a physical force and qualifiers that carry violence. The protagonist of 'Gangster' doesn't merely climb a staircase; he 'pounds the ribcage of the staircase, his footsteps thumping…'. Characters have 'massive, bull-like heads and fists of iron'. They fill up wide doorways with bodies that are like dark boulders. Bagul's sentences twist and turn through aggressive clauses or come at you like battering rams in short, blunt strokes. He is a mix of Gothic poet and expressionist painter. In his intensely experienced world, dawn breaks open the hard plateau of darkness with a crowbar to let out the sun; the shadow of a tree tries to run away, angry with the earth, but the earth will not let it escape; a disturbing event makes village peace collapse and writhe on the ground, as though bitten by a scorpion.

It is interesting to note the radical difference between how the sensitive middle-class poet-critic Shirish Pai responded to Bagul's stories and how the Dalit academic-playwright-thinker Datta Bhagat saw them. Pai, editor of *Navyug* magazine which published many of the stories in this collection, confesses in her introduction to the Marathi edition of the book that she used to experience joy mixed with fear in anticipation of a Bagul story. The joy came from knowing it would be a good piece of fiction; the fear came from not knowing what the content would be. With characteristic political naïveté and a standard notion of fiction, she asserts that Bagul's characters are perverse. This leads her to question whether a writer who creates perverse characters is himself perverse. She then proceeds to assert that although this is often so, it is not true of Bagul. He is an artist who is hungering for 'a strong, beautiful and pure world'. He is weighed down by the empathy he feels for a world gone wrong. He is brought to a standstill by the destruction of life he sees around him. Finally, when the ongoing assault on humanity becomes unbearable: '… a tempest rises in his soul. Words struggle to come out. He feels like shouting out to the world, open your eyes and ears to what is going on around you.' Pai mistakes the source of Bagul's fiction as personal emotion when it is, in fact, a clear-headed vision of what Dalit fiction should be. Also, Bagul is not addressing himself to the world, but simply putting the life of his people out there to give it a public face. He is saying, here is the world that the public has so far erased from its consciousness. Now look at it and deal with it.

As against Shirish Pai's purely literary response to Bagul's fiction, Datta Bhagat asserts its political importance. For him Bagul defines Dalit literature as a movement that runs parallel to and is a reflection of the social movement, pioneered by Mahatma Jotiba Phule, Gopal Ganesh Agarkar and Dr B.R. Ambedkar, which demanded freedom, justice, equality and brotherhood. The best Dalit writing, and Bagul's is up there in the vanguard, does not articulate its commitment to this social cause simplistically—that would make it propaganda—but is a profoundly felt response to the complexity of the socio-cultural forces that have shaped the world. Bagul's stories place characters in the very eye of this social storm in order to follow their inevitable hurtling towards ends which are often tragic but occasionally also triumphant. Placed thus, the characters are neither black nor white, certainly not perverse, but purely and simply human.

Take 'Streetwalker' for instance. Bagul does not dwell on the fact that the protagonist Girja walks the streets not out of personal choice but because she has no choice. Instead, he concentrates on her universal aspect. She is a mother who must earn enough money on that particular evening to enable her to travel to her village to see her son who is ill. In 'Prisoner of Darkness', Bagul's compassion reaches out to both Banoo, the kept woman, and her son who despises her for being what she is—both victims of social circumstances. The Ethiopian protagonist of 'Gangster' has also been a victim of exploitation and has never been loved. Suddenly, when a woman comes to him for help, he reaches into himself and finds a human being there.

We get a vivid picture of how Baburao Bagul saw his characters from an essay he wrote for the 1969 Diwali issue of *Marathwada*. 'Dalit literature believes that looking for the meaning of life in social debates, philosophy or political manifestoes would make it monochromatic. The meaning of life is to be found in Nature. Man is the very embodiment of Nature. His desires, passions, emotions are the sun, moon, rain, shine, storms and gales of Nature. When these natural desires and emotions were crushed as the shadripu or the six perverse passions of human life, religion and gods became immortal and life, which once sang hymns to Usha, the Goddess of Dawn, was incarcerated in the dark. But now we herald the coming of tempests, wildfires and light; of varied paths and triumphant chariots. The ages will come and go like birds alighting on trees, and joys will abound.'

The eleventh edition of *Jevha Mi Jaat Chorli Hoti* was published in 2013. They say translation gives a classic an afterlife. Jerry Pinto's fluent, empathetic translation has done that for this classic. When Shirish Pai published Baburao Bagul's first story, he wrote to her saying, 'My story will now live a freer life than I do.' This translation will allow his stories to spread their wings even further.

Shanta Gokhale
Mumbai

Prisoner of Darkness

THE EVENING, A woman adorned by the departing sun's warm love, proceeded to the west, and darkness fell. It was at this melancholic moment that Ramrao Deshmukh's* body was ablaze on his funeral pyre. His son Devram, bare-chested, his massive body as hard as a rock, spun around from the pyre; the heat pressing down upon the corpse's chin had caused the skull to explode, the sharp crack eliciting a wail of grief from all those who had been close to the dead man. Devram punched the air with a fist as powerful as a hammer. He gnashed his teeth and between sobs, he shouted, 'Banoo! You…'

Seeing her husband, usually as cruel and unfeeling as a tiger, lament in this extraordinary fashion, Devram's wife Kamala began to howl. And all those who had accompanied the body on its last journey, taking their cue from the demoniac Devram's grief and Kamala's howling, also began to dab their eyes with their head cloths.

---

*Deshmukh, in Marathi, means the hereditary chief, or head, of a territory—a district or a village—which was known as Deshmukhi. The system was abolished after Independence, but in parts of Maharashtra, Deshmukhs are still powerful landowners.

Their eyes might have been tearful but as they stared surreptitiously at Devram's finely muscled body, they also began to fear him a little. As soon as his father died, Devram's desire for revenge and his uncontrollable anger had brought him to a final and unalterable decision: he would murder his father's widow, Banoo. He thrust his head forward now, a buffalo lowering its horns to butt heads with a rival. The will to murder gave his body a new velocity; his back and his biceps seemed to writhe like snakes trapped under his skin.

Devram's unbridled fury frightened the members of the funeral procession even as it dragged them behind him. They were running to keep pace, but no one dared to stop him. Everyone knew of his youthful strength and hot-headedness; they had heard of the fists that could break your bones to bits. So they kept their tongues behind their teeth.

And so Devram was off, grinding the gravel of the riverbed under his feet. The fine sand cracked and crunched its complaints as he passed over it, unable to bear the pressure of his weight. The pebbles seemed to scramble out of the way to save themselves. Above them, Devram's desire for revenge raged on, growing fiercer by the second. The desire to pump any number of bullets into Banoo, a desire that had been held in check for twenty years by his fear of his father, was now in full flame. He wanted to kick her voluptuous, beautiful, tender young back; his hands itched to grab her ankle-length, silky-black hair and shake her senseless. He could not wait to get his hands on her, and this made the tramp down the road agonizing for him. The funeral followers were certain that Banoo had cast a spell over Devram; she must have worked some black magic to bewitch him, they thought; and this certainty made them hurry after Devram, ignoring the corpse on the burning pyre.

In the middle of this fear-stricken crowd was the young and slender Kamala, swathed in a silk sari, stumbling as she hurried to keep up. She was taking her life in her own hands, following her husband. The two days of weeping and fasting had left her as shrivelled as yesterday's coriander. But she struggled along, trying to keep her balance, driven as much by the unstoppable excitement of the moment as by the fear of Banoo and the fervour driving her husband. The suspicion that Banoo had set Khandoba* on her husband was a tiger gnawing at her insides.

Kamala's father was even more frightened. What would happen to Kamala now, he wondered. His rubicund and shiny head bare, his turban and his slippers under one arm, he moaned as he lumbered along. His weak feet stumbled over the stones and pebbles of the path. Now and again, he slipped a little, only to save himself. He could not stop; the love he bore his daughter drove him to risk life and limb.

The ragtag crew behind them was mumbling and muttering Banoo's name. Everyone was sure that she was an evil spirit who had taken a beautiful human form. Out of a mania for money, she had worked her magic on Devram. They were sure that Devram was going to fall over any moment, frothing blood at the mouth

---

*To set Khandoba on someone is to propitiate this God with promises and to turn him loose on an enemy.

as he died, and this made their skin crawl in delicious fear.

Then Devram broke his headlong rush and stood still, shivering as if a khavis* had scooped him up with unseen hands and swallowed him. The crowd of mourners, all of whom had had their eyes pinned on his mighty back, were forced to stop abruptly, with the result that they lost balance and fell into each other, but their eyes remained fixed, staring intently at Devram. *Now*, they thought, *now he's going to vomit blood, tear his hair, rip at his body, throw himself on the ground, roll about in pain and then die a terrible death.* On every back, every hair stood on end in terror; such terror, that life seemed not worth living. It was difficult to breathe. Devram stood there, his arms akimbo, his legs splayed, his head pointed in the direction of the village, his neck stiff as he scanned the sky. Then he gave his body a shake and like a rooster rooting in the ground, he began to look around for a suitable stone. As soon as he found one, he scooped it up and turned with a roar towards the crowd, which went very still. To avoid getting that stone in the head, they began to retreat, bending backwards, like weeds in a river. And suddenly, Kamala sat down, cradling her head in her hands. Now she tucked it between her knees and a wail erupted from her like lava from a volcano: 'Banoo, you murali**, you demon, you've destroyed me! God will do the same to you.'

---

*A khavis is a ghost, a particular entity whose venomous nature has made it a byword in colloquial Marathi.

**A murali is a girl child who is 'dedicated' to a God or Goddess. This is because there seems to be a call on the child's life, a divine call which can be manifested sometimes as knots

'Bané!' Devram roared again and again, and with the stone in his hand, he thundered off in the direction of the village.

Because he had been brought to this state by Banoo, every person began to spew the same venom at her.

'Bring that demon here. Let's strip her naked and take her in procession through the village,' said Kanhuji Patil.

'No, let's strip her naked and tie her up like a bull and whip her and lead her by the nose to the pyre,' said Satva Sonar, in a fine fury.

'Excellent idea. We'll get to see a good hot tamasha. No trace of that prostitute should remain this time. And I'll also be able to say she committed sati,' the Police Patil said, all agog to see Banoo's beauty.

'Yes, burn her,' Kulkarni snorted the words out with his snuff.

'Let's burn her,' many enraged voices echoed.

'Such witches deserve this kind of treatment. Or in this Kaliyug women will get out of hand. What Lord Vitthala has ordained, she has fouled. For twenty years she has dirtied the village. She's wreaked havoc in the Deshmukh Wada*. She's not let anyone live in peace there. She did not let Ramrao so much as leave the house. Right up to his death, he never emerged. The last heir

---

in the hair, sometimes intractable behaviour. But this route is generally taken when the family is too poor to provide for the girl child. Many muralis live in penury and are often exploited by various men.

*A wada is a traditional Maharashtrian home, generally ancestral, housing many generations and much endangered as a species.

of the house—Devram? She's driven him mad. And her own son? Daulat? She's driven him mad too. He's restless, like a wind, never stopping, wandering here, there and everywhere. All day he roams around and at night he sleeps anywhere, sometimes near the hills, sometimes near the boundaries of people's land, sometimes near the stream. If anyone questions him, he's ready to attack with an axe...' Sudama mumbled sadly and before he could even finish, Runjha interrupted with: 'Sudama, in the last fifteen days that mad fool, Daulya I mean, he must have started fifteen hundred fights. Only yesterday he went to the widow Pandu's devghar* and demanded water to drink. When he wasn't given any, he started a fight there as well.'

'Did he beat up the old lady?'

'The old lady said: I'll give up my life but I won't give you water.'

'What has happened!'

'That prostitute has ruined everything. Tomorrow every Mang, Mahar and Chamar** is going to turn up at a Brahmin's house and ask for water. The whore has soiled all notions of caste and creed,' Sudama continued to rail against Banoo.

Hearing these terrible curses, Nana, who was also boiling over with rage at all he had heard about Banoo, said, 'Why don't you all shut up? If you keep blowing

---

*A devghar is a shrine to the Gods inside a house. This has the sense of temple but it could be either. Hence I have left the original.

**Mang, Mahar and Chamar are three of India's many Dalit castes. Banoo, in this story, is a Mahar.

your horns, she'll rip off our dhotis and force us into saris. She'll emasculate us and make us clap and dance as hijras. Or she'll blind us…so just shut up.'

Frightened, Shankar shouted, 'Nana is right.'

And so the tradition-bound bunch of people—until then so ready to fall on Banoo with naked swords of rage—was suddenly chastised by fear of her powers. Over the last twenty years, the village, which had hated and despised her, had been kept quiescent by rumours of these powers. Otherwise, regardless of how besotted Ramrao had been, they would not have allowed her into the village. But she had lived proudly in the wada, feeding Ramrao with her own hands; she had caused the death of Devram's mother; she had driven other members of the family from the wada, including Devram's first wife who had gone back to her parents as she was unable to bear such terrible goings-on. Banoo had reduced Devram's second wife, Kamala, to a cipher in that house. And so the orthodox village had begun to thirst for her blood. Now they wanted to see whether Devram would live or die and their fear of Banoo kept them following him.

As Devram entered the village, however, things began to get a little more complicated. People began to duck and hide, fearing that Devram might attack them, too. They began to scuttle into houses. But Devram, turned into a devil by his rage, paid them no heed and surged forward implacably. In his head, he could see Banoo—and his father's guns. In his ears, the sound of those guns firing and Banoo's death-scream began to merge. Taken by rage as by a flood and blinded by it, he began to run. This scared the villagers enough to bring them out of doors.

Every man and woman was convinced all over again that Banoo had invoked Khandoba or cursed Devram and driven him mad, and they began to abuse her.

As he neared the wada, Devram began to jump and shout. He raced up the stairs to his father's room. Snatching up the gun hanging there, he roared, 'Bané, get ready to die!'

As someone who had loved old Ramrao more than life itself, loved him so much that she had until his death strangled her own maternal instincts and kept her son Daulat at arm's length, Banoo was sitting and weeping in her room; a Hirkani* bemoaning her sorrows, as she thought of the dark days ahead. When Devram saw her like this, confusion erupted in his head.

He could not decide whether to make Banoo pay for the suffering that had killed his mother or to make love to her. With each glance, he was seized again by a new aspect of her beauty.

Drowning in sorrow, Banoo sat still and unmoving as a rock. She did not see the violent intent in Devram's eyes, and so she had no idea that he had come there as a hunter, intent on attacking her, determined to kill her, and to destroy her reputation. She thought that he had been driven mad by grief and she began to cry all the more. Wiping her eyes, she said to Devram, in an intensely compassionate tone, 'Devram, my child, do

---

*Hirkani, the story goes, was a milkmaid, who got locked into the Raigad Fort. She hears her baby crying and she braves a terrible and difficult climb down the battlements to feed her child, thus earning Chhatrapati Shivaji Maharaj's respect and turning herself into a metaphor for the power of maternal love.

not despair in your sorrow. My son Daulat is mad. I am not asking for anything for me or for him. I'll leave with just the clothes I have on my body...' The hiccupping sobs would not let any more words come out of her mouth.

'You're not to go anywhere. And don't call me Devram. I am older than you. And...'

'My dear son, even if you are older in years, I was still your father's wife. A man's wife is the mother of his child. What does it matter if I am of a different caste?'

'Don't call me "son". I won't let you go... Instead of roaming the streets, whipping your handkerchief around and singing*, stay here, be my keep...'

'Devram, son—'

'I am a Deshmukh. I am not the son of some streetwalker, some shameless low-caste woman, some murali. Prostitutes don't have sons; they only have bastards...'

'Watch your mouth!' Anger and fear electrified Banoo. She began to look for a place to run but she could not see any.

And at that point, from her heart, there arose a scream for help—'Daulat!'

'Devram, for the love of God and dharma, keep calm. Don't ruin everything by letting sorrow drive you mad.' She was beginning to lose control of herself as she sought a way to get out of his clutches.

Just as she said this, Kamala burst into the room, desperate to know whether her husband had fallen dead

---

*This refers to the tradition by which muralis walk the streets, singing and waving handkerchiefs.

or had been turned blind; and Banoo screamed a plea for help: 'Kamala, save me...'

'She? Save *you*? Here, give me your sari.' Devram ran to grab Banoo by the hair and pull her to the ground so that he could strip her naked. Kamala rushed forward and threw her arms around Devram's waist so that she could prevent him from being blinded by some black magic spell. Banoo took the opportunity to run for her life, using the door that led to the gallery, into the next room, and down the stairs from there.

'Let me go!' Devram shouted and when he realized that although he had pulled the trigger the gun had not fired, he threw it aside and freed himself from his wife. He pushed her away with such force that she reeled and fell.

By that time Banoo had raced down the stairs and into the gully in front of the house. Seeing her terror, the people outside fell back and let her pass. And now the good and the great of the village began to climb the stairs* so as to see what calamity might have come to pass. They saw Kamala on the floor, insensible, and Devram loading the gun with cartridges. His terrible face, resembling that of Yamraj, the God of Death, discouraged them from asking him any questions.

Outside, Banoo, who had never descended the stairs in all the twenty years she had lived in the wada, was

---

*It is likely that the poor and the downtrodden might well have also wanted to know what was going on but would be prevented from entering the Deshmukh Wada since they would pollute it. It is therefore not the infidelity of the Deshmukh that upset the village so much as his bringing his 'untouchable' Mahar mistress into his home.

running, lost to all sense of decency, in order to protect her life and character. And at the doors, on the terraces, in the lanes, they stood, in groups, watching her run, surprised at her behaviour but also taking in her beauty. Her state left them stunned.

'Hot stuff!' someone exclaimed, breaking the spell of oppressive solemnity that had been cast by Banoo's terrified beauty. Now the poison inside them began to flow. Banoo's body responded as if flicked by fire. She immediately pulled the edge of her sari over her head—which only caused a cloudburst of lewd laughter.

The sight of her sleek, graceful midriff aroused Nana to comment, around a chew of tobacco that he almost swallowed: 'Look at how the sari slithers between her legs. Such style...'

Suka, hearing this description, said loudly: 'Devram must have had his way with her and left her like that. Someone like me would have known how to use her as a wife should be used...'

His wife said from within, 'You're no better than a beast. She's a murali. What's *your* excuse?'

'What rubbish you talk! Is she a lady like you? A woman even? She's a demoness and we should all get some of her.'

Every onlooker offered his share of scorn. Banoo was running for her life, a bird maddened by the forest fire of their words. To combat with her own voice the firebombs of their condemnation, she would ululate: 'Daulat!'

And this though she knew that there was no hope that Daulat would come to her rescue. For he had taken her to be his enemy right from birth and did not let so much as her shadow fall upon him. If she called him to her, or even spoke in tones of maternal love, he got angry. When his anger got out of control, he hit her. Once, he had even tried to murder her. That was how much he detested her. He saw her as a sinner. So she did not have much hope of him saving her from this mob. He might lead them in their taunts and abuse; perhaps he might even keep his promise—he might try once again to murder her, laughing as he made the attempt. She shivered at the thought and ran on.

'Banoo, take that…' One of the terrible curses hit her with the impact of a buffalo head-butting her. She bowed her head; and another great burst of scalding laughter poured down upon her.

'Daulat!'

'Slut, whore, a woman like you has not been born in all the three worlds. And one is not likely to come along again either. You drove your own son mad because of the sin of his birth. When you got pregnant again, you thought your husband might stray and so you had an abortion. Now bear the fruit of your sins,' an old woman cursed her; and Banoo, looking at her, began to cry. Her lips trembled with the desire to reveal the sorrows of her heart. As she opened her mouth to begin, the woman shouted, 'Begone. Or that demon will come to haunt my Ramu. Go!'

'Aaho, aatyabai*, don't talk to her like that, she might curse us,' said the old woman's daughter-in-law, drawing her sari protectively over the child at her hip.

---

*The sister of one's father is one's atya but it is a term that may be used to indicate respect for any senior lady.

That hurt Banoo more than the old woman's words. She began to run again.

As she ran, the twenty years she had spent in the wada unspooled before her eyes. In those years, she had never once been a real mother. Her only existence had been as Ramrao's lover, an object of lust. Each day of Daulat's childhood turned into a demon now, dancing before her eyes, hurting her dreadfully with accusations of neglect. Her life was burning, her guilt was screaming: 'Daulat!'

At the doorways of their homes, people heard her screams. Not one of them felt the least sympathy. On the contrary, the more she screamed, the more vitriolic was their abuse.

Banoo knew that Daulat was no fool, no idiot child. Behind his violent temperament, she began to see each of the blood-soaked secrets he had concealed. Even though she was his mother, she had done this to him: subjecting him to the evil atmosphere of the wada and the tradition-encrusted village where from childhood the constant pecking at him, the constant cawing and croaking to which he had been subjected, had all conspired to drive him mad. The insults had warped his mind. The contempt had sealed his mouth. And enduring all this had turned him violent. This knowledge turned her into a model mother; and like a drop of water on a pan, she writhed in torment on his behalf.

'She's tired. Get hold of her. Fuck her senseless...' someone shouted from the Maruti temple.

'But what has she done? If she had all these occult powers you say she has, why would she run out here, taking her life into her own hands? She was very beautiful, but she lived with that Ramrao who was old enough to be her father…from the age of thirteen she behaved like an ideal wife. If she had wanted she could have liquidated the wada. She would not have let Daulat wander here and there like a fool, she would have put him into school and made him a suitable heir to the wada. Anyone would have given him their daughter as a wife for the love of money—'

'Rubbish. She's insatiable. When the old man was no longer enough, she had him killed off and set her sights on the son. But he drove her out on the streets.'

'True. Such women see every young attractive man as a lover.'

'What rot are you talking in God's house?'

Each word that issued from the Maruti temple stung Banoo as a scorpion might. She longed to tell the truth. She was the daughter of a poor Untouchable. When she was dedicated to Khandoba, her name had been changed to Banoo and she had been left in the temple. Many men from all walks of life, driven mad by her beauty, had begun to visit her father, carrying money. He tried to protect her from turning into the wife of ten different men at the same time or being inducted into a brothel. Intrigued by accounts of her beauty, Ramrao went to see her and he finally bought her with money and the promise that she would be his alone. In order that he might not lose interest in her and turn her out of doors—where she would have to be wife to ten different men at the same time, satiating each one's lust—she danced to Ramrao's tune. But she also made him dance to hers. And so she did the things she did: so that Ramrao would not get angry, she paid no attention to baby Daulat; and in order to prevent other babies from coming along, she had her tubes tied on Ramrao's orders. All this so that her own life might not be destroyed and Ramrao's powerful lust should not find another object.

No one knew any of this. How could they? In the last twenty years, she had never appeared in front of any of them. They should have sympathized with her and held Ramrao accountable; instead, the hidebound village felt only contempt for her; they wanted her to get what they thought she had coming to her.

'Get her, you...' a voice roared from the temple.

'Let's grab her,' other excited voices joined in.

'I'll get her.'

So saying, Kashinath jumped out of the temple of the God who had set Lanka on fire for Sita's sake. A storm of screams and whistles broke out and the cacophony swallowed the village. Everyone joined the chase. Women took refuge in their homes and closed the doors. Some men were shouting, 'Stop her, stop her.' But no one seemed to have the courage to step forward and lay hands on her. Only an old woman pursued her, shouting curse after curse. Another woman, standing like a pole in the door of her house, was spurring her on.

'Kaashya, tear off her sari. The low-born woman thought she could become the Deshmukh's wife. Get her...'

'Watch out. He's coming...'

An uproar arose at the Deshmukh Wadi and at the Mulaan Wadi.

Kashinath turned to see what the matter was and Daulat's gupti* slammed into his stomach and came out the other side.

'Kashinath, pimp!'

Banoo, who had been trembling all this time with fear at the sight of Devram and his gun, was driven mad by maternal love now, and throwing out both her arms in front of her spent body, she shouted, 'Daulat!'

'Murder! Murder!'

'That madman Daulat has murdered Kashinath...'

Cries erupted from around the Maruti Temple. And several people hurried down the steps to get hold of Daulat.

'*Get back*, monkeys!' Devram appeared, roaring mightily, and they all rushed back into the temple.

'Daulat,' Banoo sprang forward, a mother intent on protecting the child who had been driven mad as much by an endless stream of poisonous abuse as by her neglect. As Daulat waved the bloodied knife, his ghastly countenance brought back memories of the violence in his eyes when he had sought to kill her. Then she saw Devram rushing at her, and the maternal love denied for years surged up in her again and she went forward. Now she felt no fear at all, neither of the death she saw in Daulat's face, nor of the demonic shadow on Devram's. When her sweaty hands reached her son's shoulders, he gripped her by the throat and threw her away from him. She fought to regain her balance and then surged forward again, borne

---

*A gupti is a dagger, generally concealed in a walking stick or cane.

on a wave of love. Daulat stepped back. Waving the knife again, he roared: 'Chandaalini, get back! Do not touch me, not even if I'm dying. I want to die.' Before anyone could realize that he had opened his mouth and spoken for the first time, he clenched his lips again and tautened his body which had longed for a mother's touch and words of love. So that the yearning for her that he had felt through his childhood might not fill him with a sudden hunger, he moved away, forcing his feelings into the furnace of his heart. Hearing his hate-filled words, the flood of love receded inside Banoo. She stepped back. They were now encircled by men holding bamboo sticks. Mother and son were circumscribed by cautious men, whose sticks controlled their movements.

And right in front of Daulat, Devram, shamelessly intent on raping Banoo, began to stroke her back. Then his hand inserted itself under her arm, and came to rest, like a snake, where Daulat had once sucked life-giving sustenance, and there it began to move and writhe.

The other hand too slithered into her armpit as Devram tried to drag her down. She struggled to free herself, she begged him to let her go. She cried out to her son too:

'Daulat my son, save me.'

But he was as motionless as a rock, simply looking at her. The expression on his face did not change. His eyes were unmoving. His hands dangled by his sides, useless as sticks. Seeing him in this scarecrow state, Devram surmised that this boy, now seventeen or eighteen, was frightened of him. And so the desire to rape Banoo grew. As he began to drag and push her down, she screamed, 'Daulat!'

'Fool, moron, coward, look now at your mother,' Devram screamed and slammed Daulat on the chest. Daulat rocked back on his heels, an image made of sawdust; then he regained his balance.

As Devram turned to lower himself to the ground, the knife in Daulat's hand glittered in the darkness and slid into Devram's rock-solid back and in the next moment, with a jerk, it came out and went in again. Afraid that they would be the next victims of Daulat's gupti, the crowd began to rain blows on his head as if they were drumming. His rage-filled, hate-soaked blood began to fly here and there.

'Aa...' he said, and before he could complete the word 'Aai' his stricken life began to mingle with the night that had now slipped away to the East.

'Aai...'

Mother.

As she bore the ignominy and shame—as she would to the end of her life—Banoo slipped her arm out from under Devram's body and struggled to prise the knife out of Daulat's fist. Her blouse was in tatters; her sari, clenched between her teeth, was torn. A curtain of black hair flowed past her shoulders. And her hand struggled to free the knife from Daulat's grasp. There was blood everywhere.

The gully was silent, the village still. The image of Maruti, which faced the village, hands folded in the flickering light of the lamp placed before it, sometimes appeared angry and sometimes sad.

Bohada*

'I, DAMU, THE village Mahar, demand that we have a sōng**, and that too a Narasimha sōng!'

This announcement caused the village to reel in shock. The peace of the village began to stagger around as if it had been bitten by a scorpion. The brilliant red statue of Lord Maruti took on a wrathful aspect, the glass lantern went silent, and at the village square, and beyond it, words began to gather and cluck.†

---

*From *Baluta* by Daya Pawar (Granthali, 1978; English translation, Speaking Tiger, 2015 by Jerry Pinto): 'I saw my first Bohada in Aurangapur. It was danced around a Holi bonfire. The dancers painted themselves as characters from the Ramayana and Mahabharata. Their faces were covered by ferocious masks, and on their backs they had circular frames of bamboo and straw… To play the role of Raavan was a big honour, for one had to manage his ten heads. One had to make a big donation to secure that role. Mahar boys were not allowed to participate.'

**A sōng is a religious masque.

†In the villages of Maharashtra, as in villages everywhere else in India, Brahmins and other upper castes lived in the centre of the village—which was also where the temples were built—and the 'polluting' outcastes like the Mahars lived on the outskirts. The area was known as Maharwada. Such segregation, though now illegal, continues in many parts of rural and small-town India.

Anger began to rule as Raavan had ruled in Lanka. Bhagwan Deshmukh's pendulous round cheeks began to vibrate. Jagannath cracked his hunter and began to curse. Raghu Arighala began to abuse even as he tried to twist his Brahminical pig tail, his shendi, into a knot. Karim Chacha began to pluck white hair from his beard and ask questions.

Through it all, there in the village gateway, at the edge of the square, stood six-foot Damu, a warrior, adamantine in colour and in body. He kept looking at the people in the square. On his face was the peace and the restraint of a powerful man.

'Go on, Maharaj...' Ganpatrao Patil, the village headman, began to say, as per protocol. But the words locked themselves up, even as his hands danced in the air, confusing things further.

'If Mahars cannot do the sōng, then who rules here?' Damu asked.

This religious sentiment put the villagers in a quandary. Then Jagannath scraped up enough energy to say, 'Hey, Damya, since when have *you* turned into the Deshmukh, donkey-spawn...' and followed this up with a torrent of abuse. Jagannath always felt that he should be acknowledged as Shamrao Deshmukh's son; that Bhagwan should accept him as his half-brother; that he should have right of residence in their wada. Of course, none of this had happened; people called him a member of the cow-herding colony, which was why this fatherless boy was always angry.

'This kind of thing, these out-of-the-way religious practices, will never happen here.' Bhagwan Deshmukh's words took the scenic route around the square before they were heard. He was a schoolteacher, and every day he abused his father, Shamrao, who had left him with nothing but the dilapidated wada. Everything else had been spent on women and wine.

'*Kinv nahin hoga? Honaach maangta!*' ('Why not? It has to happen!'), said Karim Chacha, who out of habit took a contrary position to any taken by Bhagwan. His ancestral property had been expropriated by Bhagwan's ancestors and was still a matter pending before Ganpatrao.

'Eh Daadiwala*, shut up,' Jagannath bit off bitterly and began to clench the hunter which he used only in fights and beatings.

'There is no shastrik basis for such a sin,' Raghu Arighala said as he finally secured his shendi into a topknot, albeit somewhat askew, and then ducked his head to seek proof in the *Puranas*.

'Damu *must* have a sōng,' said a dark young man aggressively.

'Why?' the village square asked, a hundred mouths as one.

The dark man hesitated but then drawing on some reserves of inner strength, he said, 'He is one of us.'

'Oh? And how is that? Is he your neighbour? Your relative?' Bhagwan began, but Jagannath cut in, turning to the dark man: 'Your house must have a bone dump**

---

*Daadiwala, literally 'bearded man', is generally a derogatory reference to Muslims.

**Having a boneyard or bone dump or haadki implies that the person must be a Mahar, an outcaste who traditionally skinned dead cattle, besides being required to perform other menial tasks. A Kunbi would not like to be called a Mahar and so this is an insult.

inside, mustn't it, Kunbata*?'

This made Ganpatrao angry. He was a Kunbi himself. He gestured to the dark young man, and to control him and placate the crowd, he said, 'People, let us at least listen to Damu.' He waved his beringed hand to the rhythm of his words and for a second, he looked at Damu with the gaze of someone who has done him a favour. The chiselled line of his moustache shone with the pride he felt at this, and he pressed the golden frames of his spectacles down on his nose though there was no need to.

'We should listen? To this pretence, this arrogance… to this haughtiness? This irreligiousness? No, friends, this will never happen.' Happy that he had firmly denied Ganpatrao Patil's suggestion, Bhagwan crossed one leg over the other with a flourish and placed an ankle on a knee. His stomach settled into his lap.

'Dada, you haven't understood,' Jagannath snapped. Every time Bhagwan spoke, Jagannath would try to interrupt him or prove him wrong, and each time he was forced to swallow some serious insults.

Now the crafty Ganpatrao said, as if handing a flaming torch to a monkey, 'Calm down, Jagannath, calm down.' His hand rose and fell with the rhythm of his voice and his many years of experience murmured: *Soon Damu will feel the lash of the hunter.*

'I want a sōng, a Narsimha sōng, saheb,' Damu thundered, enraging the gathering, tormenting Raghu Arighala, incensing Jagannath and causing a storm to brew in the village square.

---

*Derogatory term for a Kunbi.

'But where will you have it?' Ganpatrao asked, with the cunning of a fox, seeking to add fuel to the fire.

'In the temple.'

'Which one?'

The whole village square rose with a roar. Lakshya Pujari's body puffed up like grain that has been roasted. Words failed him at this blasphemy, and his body began to shake; he waved his hands about in the air. Raghu Arighala vented his rage on his hapless hair. Jagannath rustled about, hissing like a snake in the undergrowth. Bhagwan scrubbed at his foot.

'This one.'

As a bullock is turned upside down to drive shoes into its hooves, Damu's utterance overturned the village. The honest man inside Karim Chacha cried out, '*Ay kabhi hoga nahin, main aisa satyaanaash honeku doonga nahin*.' ('This will never happen; I will never let such a calamity be visited upon us'). And at the very same moment, Jagannath rose, a veritable demon, intent upon the destruction of Damu. Lightning flashed in his eyes, his eyebrows rose high, and his upper lip stretched itself into a thin line. He gnashed his teeth, the hunter hissing in his hand, as he made his way towards Damu.

In a rage, Lakshya Pujari began to scratch Lord Maruti's feet. Raghu Arighala lowered his outraged head and let his topknot come undone.

'Remember Ram Kund, people, remember Ram Kund*,' Bhagwan shrieked a warning. 'This Mahar wants

---

*In 1930, Dr Babasaheb Ambedkar staged a satyagraha at Ram Kund, Panchavati, Nashik, to get Dalits admitted into the temple.

to reduce the village to ashes. But I...' His rage did not let him complete the sentence. He could only rub his foot until his hands began to burn.

'Jaggu, stop there!' Damu's voice was like a stone flung at the feeble chest of Jagannath and it momentarily stopped the easily angered man.

'Get back, baba,' Chintya Koli shouted a warning, seized by terror. But the maddened Jagannath did not like it. When he was in the square, he did not respect the elderly. He got even angrier and shouted harshly at Damu: 'Come here, you scoundrel, shut your filthy mouth...' These abuses were half-sputtered and half-swallowed.

The overheated village square laughed out loud. That enraged the proud Jagannath further. 'Don't show your teeth like monkeys. I'll break all your teeth, each one of you.' The rage and the ridicule and the lack of food had combined to swell his face up.

Ganpatrao, the Patil, waved his hands upon the air to calm the agitated crowd—

'People!'

This time Karim Chacha did not think to oppose him. And Jagannath breathed a sigh of relief. And Bhagwan thought: *If Damu were to knock the Patil over right here and now, we would have to pretend we did not see it happen.*

'Damu,' Ganpatrao Patil said now, rubbing his nose with his fingers. Alerted to a new development, the crowd moved forward.

Waving a finger adorned with a golden ring, the Patil said, 'You should get the sōng.' And turning a meaningful eye on the crowd—to remind them of the negotiations that had taken place earlier that afternoon to bypass the

Collector's intructions—he added, 'But it will cost two hundred rupees.'

The Patil was delighted at how skilfully he had handled the situation. The people were happy at the Patil's insurmountable challenge. They were no longer frightened.

Damu began to think. He opened the doors of his poverty-stricken world and peered in: there were three lives to consider, his wife, his mother and his buffalo.

He said softly but with determination: 'I'll find the money.'

The Patil's face fell.

'Not two hundred. *Three* hundred and *only* three hundred,' shouted the crowd in the square, from its collective gut. And from the square and from outside, words flew about like stones in an angry exchange.

'How much do I give, Rao saheb?' Damu asked simply and quietly; and the entire square turned to look at him.

Raghu Arighala said: 'We're done for! This fellow will lead us to our ruin.' And Karim Chacha said, 'And why? Is he my mother? He's a dheda, a low caste…' Bhagwan agreed with Karim Chacha and he said to Ganpatrao: 'Maharaj, don't say just anything that comes to your mind.' And seeing Raghu with his head down and his shendi straggling again, he added, annoyed: 'At least cut that off!'

Damu asked again: 'How much, Rao saheb?'

Ganpatrao Patil did not like the question. But still he said in his high-bred way: 'Two hundred. Tomorrow. All of it.'

And this time he looked at Jagannath but the latter did not react.

* * *

Crossing the broken-down village gate, the next night, Damu was back in the village. The Maharwada* had made complete preparations for the expected fight.

Matching Maruti eye to eye, chest to chest, arm to arm, Damu stood in the doorway with a thick stick in his hand, the handle of an axe. And in his pocket he stroked the blade of the axe, as he looked at the crowd in the square.

'So, Damu?' Ganpatrao Patil put the question to Damu as was established practice. There was mockery in his voice, an invitation to the others to ridicule the upstart. He did not want the night-long bohada to happen.

'Damya Kaji, the big sheth is not here to give you two hundred…' said Jagannath, twisting his hunter and cursing.

'When he doesn't have the money to eat, how is he going to find the two hundred?' someone said with a harsh laugh.

'*Arre oh dheda*,' Karim Chacha's son, the tange-wala, sniggered.

'If you couldn't find the money, say so and be done,' Bhagwan said, happily massaging the foot in his lap. He did not even use Damu's name.

'If a child pees on your thigh, you don't cut it off, do you?' someone asked.

---

*See third footnote on page 19.

Jagannath cursed again. Now sarcasm had free play in the village square. The Patil's measured amusement had put a fearless stamp of approval on this.

The Collector's rule was about to be destroyed. The excitement grew.

'Damu!' the Patil said, showing some respect. 'Shall we leave?' he asked, waving his hand to indicate the crowd.

Immediately Jagannath rose and said to everyone: 'Come on folks, on your feet. The meeting has ended.'

'I have the money.'

The whole square fell into a total and complete silence. Everyone felt that it would have been better if they had got to their feet immediately when Jagannath, that mad Jagya, had.

'Show it then.'

'Here it is, Rao saheb.'

But as Damu stretched out his hand, Yanku Kothula shouted: 'Wait! I bid five hundred.'

'If someone is giving five hundred, take it!' Karim Chacha shouted in a roar that came from his gut.

'Yes, take his money,' Bhagwan growled.

'One should not let go of Laxmi's sari,' said Raghu, rising to his feet, empowered by his memory of this line from the scriptures.

And through the village square, the cry went up: 'Take the five hundred, take the five hundred!'

'Rao saheb…' Damu exclaimed in protest, and this blew some life into the rule of law, as the crowd was reminded of the Collector. The uproar settled down again. But it enraged Jagannath. 'M'haara! Shut up!' he hollered, an axe-sharp attack.

Paying no attention to him, Damu asked: 'What was said, Rao saheb? What was agreed upon?'

'What was said has fallen into the well of Bhairoba.' Jagannath's voice, laden with the curses he had flung around, was an invitation to violence.

'Doesn't matter whether a lakh was agreed upon, the sōng will go to the one who pays the most,' Bhagwan pronounced his opinion, rubbing his feet.

Lakshya Pujari nodded to show that he agreed with the schoolteacher.

'Not so easy, Patil. You will have to keep your word,' Karim Chacha said, blindly opposing Bhagwan, as usual.

'We will not break our word, nor will we behave blindly,' Ganpatrao Patil declared, shrewdly.

'*Isku bolta hai bol.*' ('This is called keeping a promise!') Karim Chacha said.

Raghu remembered the previous afternoon's scheming, while his hand went up to his shendi.

The crowd felt victorious and a collective cry of celebration went up.

Jagannath's hunter whipped through the air.

Bhagwan felt the Mahar was going to claim that the Patil had opposed the Collector's instructions.

'Rao saheb, I'll give five hundred,' said Damu. He had understood their strategy only too well.

Like a fire that was about to consume everything, Yanku growled: 'Five hundred and fifty from me, then.'

'Squashed!' Jagannath said.

'That's done it!' added another, with a laugh.

'Monkeys should not weave ropes; they may make

their own nooses,' said Raghu, twisting up a tale from the *Panchatantra*.

With victory almost a taste in his mouth, Lakshya Pujari turned to look at the Patil, his eyes fond.

Before Damu could say anything further, a dust-storm erupted: 'Folks, this is over,' Jagannath shot up and urged everyone to leave.

'Damya!' Karim Chacha began, just to provoke him.

'If you talk any more, your tongue will fall out,' Raghu swore.

'My wrist has absorbed much ghee over the years...' said Damu, holding up the stick and waving it forcefully before him.

'Waah, a brave man,' a farmer exclaimed, pleased by Damu's show of strength. No one opposed what he had said but no one supported it either.

Offering the appearance of one making a retreat, Damu now said: 'Make Yanku write it down that he'll give that much.'

'I will write it,' said Yanku and the entire village square came to life with a roar. The Patil was rather pleased at his own skilful manoeuvres. Bhagwan felt that he might have been foolish to oppose the Patil. Karim Chacha feared he may have shown his hand to the schoolteacher.

'Wait a moment, folks...' Bhagwan said, seeing that everyone was now rising to go. He wanted to oppose the Patil still, and he wanted to please Yanku by making a speech about him.

'Today, a brave man like Yanku has stood up and saved the honour of the village...'

Yanku swelled up with pride. He had had this greatness thrust upon him, however. As the crowd were slowly lowering themselves to the ground again, Damu's dark and rumbling voice rolled out: 'Six hundred from me.'

And the festival of victory came to an abrupt halt again. Bhagwan's little speech fell to bits and had to be covered with a blanket. Raghu's crafty plans were borne away on the wings of Vedanta. Jagannath's rage made him a buffalo that began to paw and stamp the ground. The Patil began to hunt for words but he could not find any. Karim Chacha's beard began to wither. The carriage driver wondered why they didn't just fight it out among themselves.

'He's just being stubborn,' Chacha said simply.

'He has it in for the village, come hell or high water,' said another.

'It's the malign influence of Shani,' said Raghu. Hearing this, Lakshya Pujari put his head on Lord Maruti's feet and began to beg him to break Damu's head.

The Patil, pressing his fingers on the bridge of his nose, began to think deeply.

Bhagwan tried, with a series of gestures, to encourage Yanku to speak. Jagannath used the energy of abuse to spur him on; and with the help of all this pushing Yanku said reluctantly: 'Seven hundred fifty.'

'Take it in writing,' Damu said immediately and to show he was ready to go, he began to stroke the blade of his axe.

Still not alert to what was going on, Ganpatrao said: 'I'm taking it.' Hearing this, Yanku said hurriedly: 'I don't want the sōng and I don't want the bohada either.' And without looking at anyone, he descended the steps and said, 'Some game you played there, Patil.'

'My six hundred...' Hearing Damu speak, the Patil began to rub his nose. Jagannath could not get up from his place. Bhagwan's hands were immobile. Raghu's hands could not get to his hair. Karim Chacha, his beard gripped in one hand, stared at the diyas on the threshing floor.

'Mahars are spreading like a forest fire,' someone said.

'Well done, Veera,' the dark boy leapt up and bore Damu away. It seemed to everyone as if Lord Maruti had abandoned his temple.

* * *

The bohada began. The sambal began to play. Ganpati began his performance, his head nodding. *Dance Sarjabai* was danced to the rhythm of the kaand, decorated with peacock feathers.

Two men formed the body of Marutiraya and took long leaps and strides. Ram and Lakshman danced forward and backward, hand in hand.

And wearing the mask of Narasimha was Damu. Coconuts were broken. Limes were cut. And slicing through the heart of darkness, roaring with all his might, danced Damu. He danced, he fought and in a state of rudra, divine rage, he shook the village to the foundations.

'We haven't had a Narasimha like that in twenty years—' Karim Chacha said to an old man.

And the Patil was saying: 'Now we should have no more bohadas.'

And the Mahars were saying, 'Next year, we will dance as the five Pandavas. And then let them bring down death or destruction, it will be all the same to us.'

Streetwalker

GIRJA HAD VISITED Haji Malang in the night. The next morning, she got up and washed and then called out to the people who she knew would take the prasad she had brought to distribute. Then she went off to get herself breakfast. She had saved some prasad to distribute among those she would meet there as well. After breakfast she planned to wash the clothes she had worn to the hill of Haji Malang. She was going to scrub her body with soap and coir until it foamed and frothed. And then in the evening, she'd eat some paan and go out to work to earn some good money. She was no longer worried about the new girl. She had prayed to Baba for herself and she had prayed that her competition should be ruined. Now she had left it all to Him. Everything would now go as she wanted it to go. She had so many blessings from so many fakirs. She had fed one of them for a full two days. She had been open-handed in giving alms. She had spread a chadar over Baba's grave. She had fulfilled every ritual in the prescribed manner and with complete devotion; and she was sure her devotion would bring her success in her trade. This was an article of faith with her.

And so it was with a light step and a bright smile that she tripped up the stairs and into the restaurant. Excitedly she squealed, 'Kaasam, here's prasad…'

The surly restaurant owner who was tired of giving Girja credit beckoned her over but Girja did not get up from her chair. Instead, she fired off her order.

The restaurant owner had enough of this haste. He got angry and shouted: 'Telegram.'

Girja pushed her chair back abruptly and shouted, 'Telegram?'

The restaurant owner explained the contents of the telegram to her calmly. Girja began to wail and weep. She threw herself at his feet, begging him for a loan so she could go to the village.

Unimpressed by her grief and tears, he said: 'I held on to the wire for two days. I did not throw it away in the waste paper. On top of that, I allowed a woman like you to use my address. That's enough favours. Go now. I've given you a lot of credit already.'

With nothing left to say, she went out. Every cell of her body was ripe with grief but she began to get ready to go to work.

Working up some foam with the soap, she scrubbed her face. Then she dried it on her dirty blouse. She set the mirror in front of her, and the sight of her face undid the control she had exercised over her tears. The sobs burst from her; the mirror dropped from her hand. She cried and cried and did not stop until her mind grew quiet; then she applied herself again to the task of beautifying herself. She oiled her hair and parted it. She pulled it back into a loose bun. She freed a lock and let it dangle along one side of her face. She put a spot of kumkum on her forehead. She took off her blouse and pulling the ends together, she tied them around her chest. She took off her sari and turned it inside out and tied it tight around her waist, arranging it so that it would show off her back. Then swaying on her high-heeled slippers, swinging her hips deliberately, she stepped out of her hut. After much pleading, she managed to get some paan-supaari on credit. But even as she made up a paan, her fingers felt oddly reluctant. Nor did she feel like eating the paan but she forced herself to chew it so that the betel-juice might redden her lips. But for some reason, it did not work; her lips would not redden. Her face would not brighten. Her mind would not lighten. Her gait had no spring in it. There was no sparkle, no spark to her. For her heart was sad. Her unhappiness was spilling out of her. It only seemed to grow greater with every step she took to control it. She felt she had lost her mind after hearing the news in the telegram; all her previous excitement had oozed out of her.

Broken by sorrow, she went and stood near the garden. This had been her beat for several years now; but no one familiar was there. With a dry mouth, she chewed her paan, hoping to brighten her lips. She went to the tap and splashed her face with water, hoping to wash away the sorrow writ large there but it would not go. The men would not turn to look at her; and though she wanted to cry, she could not give herself leave.

She smiled at the men she saw. She made use of all the tricks of the trade to incite men's lust but to no avail. Not one man came up to her. No one even asked her what she would charge. Time was slipping away, the men were slipping away. No one had any respect for her sorrow. It seemed to her the day was a dungeon and the men had locked her in it.

And then suddenly she saw him. He had been speaking to an old woman and was now looking at her. As he came closer, her heart began to thump. Sweat broke out all over her body. All the terrible things he had done to her when they were alone came back as scorpion-sting memories. He was close now. He was going to say something. If he spoke, she could not refuse. She would have to go with him. She would have to do whatever he asked. She would have to pretend to enjoy his ravages. She did not know what to do. She could not figure out how to escape his clutches.

She was scared.

He came up to her, walked past her…and was gone. Her trembling seized. His large white back turned into darkness in front of her eyes. For a long time, she simply stood there. When she came back to her senses, she felt it would have been better if she had said something, smiled perhaps. She could have snagged him and it would have hastened her departure to meet her son. She began to move forward, but her voice would not emerge from her throat. His savagery was a ghost that still had the power to terrify her. She turned back and ran to the old woman.

'Ay, old hag, don't send any girls to that one…'

'Why not?' the old lady asked, without looking at Girja.

'Because I say so…' Girja said angrily.

'Mind your own business,' said the old lady, spurning Girja's selfless concern; and Girja, shivering with anger, went and threw herself under a tree, muttering abuse under her breath.

The tree's shadow was angry with the ground and kept moving away from it. But the ground was reluctant to let it go. Girja lay there, under the tree, her stomach hurting with hunger. But like the shadow, her mind was dumb and still wanted to run away.

'Girja!'

Seeing Narayan Shetty standing before her, she forced herself to rally in mind and body. Now she was sure of an acquisition. He would take her. Her time of worry and woe would be over. For he would bring two men with him, they would treat her like a human being, they would not add to her pain.

Or so she had decided. She could not let a customer like Narayan go. She could not let her pain increase. She would not allow herself to weep. In a moment, she was a beauty, performing the rites of self-adornment, a woman from one of Saganbhau's lavanis. She ran her hands over her face and cracked her knuckles against his forehead.

'Where have you been all these days?'

The mother in her wanted to confide in him: 'My child is ill. I got a telegram. And I don't have a paisa.' But she was alert enough to slay the impulse to be human. It might drive him away and she could not afford to drive a single client away. Once again, she rallied her skills. She simpered. She fussed and frolicked and even as she faltered, she laughed with all she had in her and said: 'I was not to be touched.'* She knew that once you say that,

---

*She means she was in a state of ritual impurity; she was menstruating.

the clients stop fooling around. They don't haggle over prices. They don't argue about charges and they take you at the price that you ask. And her arrow found its mark.

'Waah,' Narayan exclaimed.

'Five rupees,' she raised the price of her body, seeing that he was losing control.

'Five?'

She was going to get some five-rupee clients. And she would take the night train to the village. To extract five rupees from his pocket, she began to play off all her tricks. She acted flustered, embarrassed. She said coyly, in a low voice, 'You're the first one, after the…' And then she let her body droop, as if lifeless, an offering she was making of her eagerness.

He kissed her and lifted her up and held her, asking, 'Is that the truth?'

Since he did not seem to have believed her words, she tried some special moves and gestures and managed to convince him to come back to her. Though she was still unhappy, she began to feel some happiness. Having showed herself to be intimate with him, she had advertised her trade effectively; she had been seen by many people. She was now sure she would get at least three or four more clients. But even after a long time, no one came along. Time was passing; her hunger increased. Her sadness began to increase too and she felt she was going to cry at the day's merciless unfolding. She was angry too. She despaired. In a rush, she decided to give up. She came out of the garden but then she turned back again. Her mind was a candle in a storm. She worked at calming it down and at finding Narayan Shetty. Now she had run out of time. She would take on whoever she got at whatever rate they offered and she would be done by twelve. She went back into the garden. She had to act intimate with Narayan Shetty again and advertise her calling as blatantly as possible.

But even after she had made several turns of the garden, he was nowhere to be seen. No one spoke to her or even looked her over so she looked flirtatiously at two pehelwans from Satara who were dawdling by the deer enclosure. Then she turned to look back and see if it had worked. Only to display the beauty of her back, she rolled up the pallu of her sari and began to wipe away the sweat. Then she began to fan herself.

'Oh fuck, look, the old hag's flirting with us,' they laughed and spat and walked off.

And so, raging at the humiliation, vanquished by hope, tormented by sorrow, plagued by ill-luck, gnawed at by hunger, maddened almost, she beckoned to a man in spectacles who was looking at her. He asked what she would charge.

'Five rupees,' she said but she had no energy left. Her body had lost its strength, it was hollow. He took her tiredness to be fear, her newness to the trade. Looking at her clothes and assessing her inexperience, he fixed a price.

'Two,' he said. Girja, confused and desperate, shook her head.

'Come,' he pretended to be in a hurry now. For he knew that if you act as if you are in a hurry, it generally settles things faster. Girja felt she now had a live one and so she began to flirt in order to warm him up.

'How long have you been doing this?'

He had come to the flashpoint.

She knew why he was asking and so she lied: 'Two months.'

'Is that all?'

She did not feel like saying any more. But to fool him and to get some more money out of him, she said: 'I wanted to be a dancer.' As she said this, she fell into the role so perfectly that he was completely taken in. All he could do was issue a single command: 'Come on.'

'First the money. You Mumbai people...' Now she had turned into a naive woman. And the mother inside her had bowed her head like a cow.

'I won't run away...'

'I won't be able to catch you,' she said, covering her head with the pallu of her sari. She began to dry the tears that had sprung up in her eyes with deceptive elegance. She pushed the sari away. Her face, every cell of it, was filled with pain with the result that he pushed five rupees into her hand and they got into a tram that was going to Foras Road*.

In order to increase his confusion about her and to get more money out of him, Girja turned herself into a model Indian woman. She suppressed her habit of talking about herself. She did not look at anyone. She kept the pallu of her sari firmly in place. She brought the edge of it down until it almost touched her nose. In her eyes was the look of a woman who had had no experience at all. She had to become, she knew, his perfect Indian woman. She clung to him as they walked. And all the

---

*A red-light area in Central Mumbai.

while, her desire to hug her child, to caress him, slashed at her like a sword. Whatever she did, that feeling was alive. It would neither die nor fade.

He? He was thinking about robbing her. Women who were new to the trade were not alert. She would have no idea how to service many clients without exhausting herself. She seemed to be a simple, pleasant woman. It would be easy to rob her; what she had could be easily taken from her.

They got off at the corner and went to a room. She went to the bedding and slumped down on it. He locked the door.

'Stand up...'

But she had decided to sit down. This was to show that she was a frightened novice. But it was also true that she did not have the strength to stand.

'Stand up,' he asked again. She shook her head. He asked again, again.

She kept refusing. This obstinacy, this refusal truly pleased him. He put a two-rupee note into her fist and stuck his hands into her armpits and hoisted her to her feet.

Each time he asked her to shed an item of clothing, she would refuse and he would insist. Each time, he would give her another two-rupee note. Then it would come off and he would ask for the next and the next and finally, she was naked and her hands were stuffed with two-rupee notes.

And then he began to have his way with her, tormenting her in whatever way took his fancy. At each new demand, he gave her another two-rupee note. She felt this was Haji Malang Baba's blessing. He gave her money willingly and she made her body into a stone and bore the terrible pain he inflicted on her. Now she not only had money to go to the village but for the medicines as well.

She gave over her body to the satisfaction of every one of his twisted desires.

But this took the last of her strength. She could bear nothing further. Her consciousness began to fade. Her fist began to loosen as if a lock were opening. The bundle of notes fell to the floor.

* * *

As if licked by a sudden flame, her body jerked. She raised her head and looked around. Her fist was empty. She rolled over and began to search the floor, sweeping it with her hands even as she lay there. Nothing. And then her gaze fell on something. The bespectacled man was getting dressed. And in the next second his duplicity became clear.

Her docile body, racked by terrible pain, pushed to the extremes of endurance, came back to life, such was the effect of the rage she felt. Her upper lip peeled back to her nose and became a straight line. In her muscles, strength began to gather. Her eyes filled with the rage of the serpent. Her face grew red with anger. She dragged the blanket into a makeshift covering and burst out: 'You pimp, where do you think you're off to? Drop that money!'

At the very door, he paused for a moment, startled by her altered avatar. He grew alert, watching her, knowing that she was about to pounce. When she did, he got her by the neck and flung her aside carelessly as one might fling a cat.

And she fell, a mother maddened by love, burned by her own sorrow, she fell and she lay where she had fallen. The fist that was holding the blanket together as if it were a sari, tightened into a lock. As a flame rises from a sacrifice when 'swaha' has been intoned and ghee has been poured, her tongue burst from its home behind the door of her teeth.

The owner of the restaurant had lied to her.

Her son had died.

He was dead.

Gangster

HE POUNDED THE ribcage of the staircase, his footsteps thumping as he walked. He struck the door with a powerful fist. The door took the blow and opened. Peace evaporated from the room behind it; it began to darken with fear. Seeing the angry demon standing there, the Bohri treasurer sitting inside began to stammer and stutter. Terror filled his eyes.

'Give me some chips.'

The Bohri man could not understand this urgency. He could not make himself get up—and this when the man outside was not willing to suffer a moment's delay.

'Quickly,' he roared.

His iron-coloured face swelled up with anger. His bone-white teeth flashed in a menacing grimace. His small red eyes gave him the look of a cruel bear from Africa.

Swallowing spit-balls of fear, the old Bohri got up and began to fumble in the cupboard. This delay further enraged the terrible man. He needed money quickly. He wanted to go and slam it down in front of Jayantiben so that he might soothe the storm in his heart.

He gave the old man a buffet and grabbed the money. He rushed out, and ran down the steps, his feet keeping pace with his racing heart. The slap of his slippers ate up the distance as this magnificent, iron-chested man, black as night, his hair curly, his face thrust forward, stormed down the road, as if he were a wild animal about to pounce on its prey.

As the road turned, a small paan shop lodged in the angry man's eye and he turned abruptly towards it.

In the broad mirror of the paan shop, four wastrels were getting nothing done in a hurry. One was using the juice of the tambul to redden his lips. The second was cleaning his face with an air of deep appreciation for his own efforts. The third was pulling the ears of his collar up. The fourth was trying to fluff his hair out to make it look a little more luxuriant. Suddenly a dark cloud appeared and the four faces vanished with the speed of startled squirrels. Only two red slit eyes in a face the colour of iron were now reflected in the mirror. The entire shop went uncomfortably dark.

'Paan...' the echoes resounded among the glass bottles. The small shop trembled. The paanwala's hands, intent on preparing a betel-leaf, jerked to a stop. His fingers which had a pinch of tobacco between them would not let it go. The rhythm of his movements had been disrupted. Darkness clouded his vision. He felt as if he had been seized by a huge monster out of a whirlwind and began to tremble.

His hands began to flutter like a bird among the bottles and jars as he selected the condiments. They reached the extreme limit of speed possible and then collapsed limply.

'Here you are,' the paanwala said, without raising his head.

One hand, rich with the virility of Africa, plunged into a pocket and came out with an inflated wallet. Tossing a coin down, the man strode off and the oppressed paanwala was left staring—an insect regarding the powerful departing back.

This mysterious man's discomfiture shocked many people. In that crowded hour, passers-by jumped out of his way. Behind him, a crowd slowed its steps even as it followed him. They were all scared that he might suddenly turn around.

'Gone,' the people heaved a sigh of relief and things went back to normal.

* * *

'Does she love me?'

This terrible cry exploded from his burning heart like a bullet out of a gun. His feelings surged and stormed, a flock of startled bats in his head. His unease increased; it was as if electric jolts were shattering his peace of mind. He felt like a wounded wild animal, frothing at the mouth.

When he saw the hutments, he stopped with the same haste with which he had been approaching it. From his uncontrollable, obsessive heart, the same cry arose: 'Does she love me?'

He was not about to receive the answer he wanted, the relief he sought. Before he had joined a gang in Hong Kong, he remembered doing an immense amount of work. After that, he had performed several bloody deeds for a blood-soaked gang with a bravery that he could still remember. He had felled his first man easily, with a single blow but what he had felt after this first murder still haunted him. During his life in Hong Kong, he had no memory of the company of even one woman. Nor did he remember his parents. He had no recollections of a mother's magical touch, of her stroking his head or back or face. He had no idea how he had ended up in Hong Kong either. He only remembered a street. And holding on to that memory, he had grown huge, as big as an elephant.

* * *

Hong Kong had become too hot for him.

Finally it had come to the point where he could no longer stay there. The law was hunting him, axe in hand. This meant he could not break out of the enfolding embrace of darkness. He could not come out during the day. The sun could not come near him. Some years passed like this. He had never found a woman. No woman had ever looked at him and smiled. Or wept. Or complained about him.

One day, the gang moved to Singapore. There too, they carried on the same activities and there too, he lived in the same dark loneliness.

There were two Chinese and two Europeans in the gang who were allowed to move around freely. They could come and go as they pleased; but he did not have permission to go out. One glimpse of him and he would be arrested and the entire gang would then be at risk.

He knew this but still one day, he did go out and just as the mynah calls its alarm when it sees a snake, the sex workers of Singapore shouted up a storm at the sight of him.

He turned back. The gang began to howl about his going out and the supervisor issued a stern order.

Despite that, the next day, he sought out the prostitutes' lane again. A German prostitute savagely and clearly turned him down on the grounds of his appearance. He tried to bribe her with a lot of money but she refused and in terrible words, she told him what had happened to another woman who had accepted a customer like him.

He turned back.

At the hideout, he and the supervisor had a fight. Both threatened to kill the other. A temporary truce was patched up but the gang had begun to turn against him. They thought to kill him and leave Singapore. He got wind of this. Finally it was he who killed the boss and left. The gang broke up. Some went to Taiwan and some came to Mumbai via Karachi.

Ten years passed. During that period no woman ever showed any sign of attraction for him. Nor did he ever visit the red-light areas. He had not forgotten the German prostitute's words. He did not want to become an animal, driven by lust. But in the night, of her own accord, Jayantiben had come to him, had sought him out. She was weeping, babbling, asking for something in Gujarati. The entire slum feared him as if he were a fiend. And yet, alone, in the night, this petite, fragile widow had stood in the house of an ogre and had had the gall to ask something of him.

No woman had ever stood so close to him. No woman had ever wept before him and in truth, he had never seen a woman at such close range. He had never experienced the effects of a woman's tears.

And then, just as the crowbar of the first rays of the sun cracks the dark boulder of the night and allows the light to flood through, her weeping broke his shell open. He agreed to help and went out to get the money.

* * *

'He's coming!' the people standing in the chowk around the bhenda tree announced, their voices filled with trepidation. They had gathered there to accompany Jayantiben's mother on her last journey.

He came forward, each stride a pounce, as he headed towards Jayantiben's hut. His backwash dispersed muck-smeared men and mosquitoes alike.

He put his hand on the poor lintel of the house and stuck his huge head in, scanning the room for Jayantiben. Seeing him, the hut lost its courage. The men looked down. The women pulled their pallus over their heads and folded their bodies into themselves. Jayantiben let loose an ululation.

Hearing this wail that Jayantiben let loose on seeing him, his heart rose on a tidal wave of feeling. He felt as if all his questions had been answered.

And in that second, the storm in his heart stopped. He felt the joy of having escaped some huge calamity. He threw the swollen packet of money in front of Jayantiben.

Men of all castes, states and religions were at work. They were getting the bier ready.

The preparations done, the corpse was raised. 'The Ethiopian' offered his shoulder as one of the corpse bearers and when the burden was settled on his shoulder, he began to walk at a crisp pace. The other three pall bearers were not as tall as he. They had to hold the bamboo rods high up with their hands as they trotted after him. They were all concerned that the body might slip and slide off the bier.

They were almost running now. Carrying the burden of the corpse and chasing the Ethiopian was proving difficult. But who could stop him? Who could tell him that the old woman's body was bouncing along in indecorous fashion? Who was going to blame him if the corpse fell?

The three of them and the people behind were now running. Then suddenly he came to a halt, looking stunned and exhausted. The other three stopped to mop their brows.

In his heart, a pain began to grind, as if deep inside him, something was being born. He might have discovered what this was if he had wept. But he had never wept in his life!

Dassehra Sacrifice

THE ENTIRE COURTYARD was glowing, beautiful, filled with people. On the steps in front of the temple, the village folks sat, and the Untouchables were in the open maidan, where they endured the warm love of the last rays of the setting sun. Some people were sitting under a tree awaiting the seema pujan*; and some were sitting in the branches of a tree. But all eyes were fixed, eagle-like, on the Maharwada. Every heart there was filled with an intense eagerness. And that eagerness was translating itself into a symbol. The symbol was the God of the Mahars and it was already growing, enlarging, becoming so big that it would soon touch the horizon. Others were thinking of the ways of the buffalo and their chests were already thundering in fear.

'Here it is,' shouted someone who, by virtue of being right where the seema pujan would be held, saw it first. All eyes strained in the direction of the Maharwada. What they did not see was a buffalo, as wild as an elephant in masth, with Shiva struggling to control him. What they did see was the Patil. He was seated on a decorated horse,

*This is a pooja performed at the border of the village.

riding it with an air. The dwarf of a horse was prancing like a decked-up hobbyhorse. On the Patil's head was a heavy crested turban, covered in embroidery, and his eyes had come to rest somewhere close to his nose. He had his head held high and his chest puffed out. He had eked out his moustaches across his thin cheeks. On his body, the copper buttons of his green coat shone forth. He had a pancha tied around his waist, a sword by his side. One hand held the reins, the other the whip and so the Patil approached the crowds that had gathered. The Mahars came foward. The balutedars* bent at the waist. Some villagers folded their hands. Some sneered. And accepting such respect as he was offered, the Patil went to the tree at the edge of the village, performed his pooja and took his usual place.

More people gathered now, to watch with felonious intent.

'Here it is,' and the whole crowd grew excited as they watched and like the pole star, their gazes were steady. Some of them felt heat pass over their bodies; for others, it was as if lightning had run over them; a thousand hands were raised and losing all control, people began to shout; some had weapons in their hands; some had ears of jowar and bajra; apta leaves** began to wave and a spark appeared in every eye.

---

*There are twelve castes, or baarah balutedars, who do not get paid for their labour but have a share in all the produce of the village. This tradition gives Daya Pawar's autobiography *Baluta* its title. (Granthali, 1978; English translation, Speaking Tiger, 2015 by Jerry Pinto).

**The leaves of *Bauhinia racemosa* are used symbolically; they generally stand for gold.

The buffalo, raised specially for the sacrifice, had been fed liquor and this had driven him mad. In his eyes, embers flickered. On his huge head, shendur had been smeared and this dripped from him. Around his muscular neck, a garland of wild flowers had been strung. As he had been shaved, his black hide glittered. Looking at the animal, everyone could tell that he was going to kill someone. Mighty Deva, using all his reserves of agility and flexibility, was slowing him down. He was slamming his body into the head of the bull. He countered each of the bull's tricks. In one hand he held the guide rein. All this meant that the animal's temper was not getting any better. In his liquor-maddened brain, he had begun to take an active dislike to Deva. Now he was intent on bringing Deva down, eviscerating him, but finding no success in these endeavours, he remained in a state of high rage. Each little thing was bringing him closer to an explosion. The noise of the crowd maddened him further. He inflated his neck and began to pour his strength into his forequarters and legs so that he might charge them and offer a fitting show of his contempt. Deva and three of his companions stopped him. This angered him further and he began to pull and buck, trying to make them lose their balance but they did not oblige.

Watching this terrifying display, the crowd began to worry about Shiva and Deva. Thoughts of death began to cloud their hearts. Shiva's father found his breath catching in his throat. Deepa Mahar had to work hard to keep bad thoughts at bay. Some of the elderly Mahars got angry with Deva. For it was on his insistence that they had brought this vehicle of the God of Death to be sacrificed.

'The animal is a monster, a pimp gone haywire; he's too much to handle,' said Deepa, gnawing on his lip.

'Deva can manage him all right,' said Ranu Chamaar, comparing the animal's ferocity and Deva's strength. 'Look at Deva.'

The crowd looked at Deva with great affection. He had a pink mulmul turban on his head. On his chest, he had an earth-red vest. This gave his lean and muscular body a most attractive line and the whole crowd began to admire the proportions of his thighs and calves, his biceps and triceps, his chest and neck. Hearing this, Shiva's father forgot his fear and asked, 'What about my Shiva?'

Black as a crow and strong as stone, his father gazed on him with admiration.

'They're like the Angadh and Maruti pair, the two of them,' said Karim Chacha.

'True, but history should not repeat itself. Only then can we see this as a victory,' said an upper-caste Maratha, digging up unwanted memories of last year's humiliation.

'Nothing like that will happen this year. Deva is there to uproot hills as Maruti once did!'

Last time, the bull had proved too boisterous for them. He had gone out of the village and into the fields of the adjoining village and the Patil of that village had claimed him, as by right.

'That isn't going to happen again. Even if you don't take Shiva and Deva into account, Hari and Kisan are also tough young men,' said Bhiva Patil, who was sucking on his thumb as he surveyed the four young Mahars who were advancing with ropes in their hands.

'But what is this nonsense? It seems as if this time Hari

won't be able to manage,' said a man who was sitting on a tree and stealthily smoking a beedi.

'He seems a bit weak and fearful,' Sheikh Ustad said.

As the buffalo approached, an unknown fear seized the Patil's heart. His face was losing lustre and vitality. As the bull tried his stunts, the crowd responded, sometimes with silence, sometimes with roars of delight. In an extraordinary fashion, they seemed to be united in body with the four Mahars who were controlling the animal, as if they shared their bodies and their exertions.

Deva stood up. The entire crowd fell silent. The ball of fear in the Patil's stomach melted away. The three of them took up positions and stopped the bull in its tracks. The animal began to struggle unsuccessfully to get away.

With his hand on the sword and leaning on his cane, the Patil came into the enclosure, trying to bring a look of calm to his face although he was terrified inside. The elders of the village accompanied him. One of the Mahars was holding up a naked sword. Another had an axe on his shoulder. A third had a basket of flowers, akula and bakula, on his head. The fourth had tied the ends of a dhotar to the back of his neck and left only a scrap in front of his tummy. The old folk and the curious kids of the Maharwada followed.

Seeing the Patil and his companions advance, the bull's ill temper got worse. His eyes were bloodshot. The effect of the alcohol was increasing. The Patil's fear grew. Words would simply not emerge from his mouth. He got angry at the young men but could not say anything. Keeping an eye on the bull, the Patil approached and came to stand beside him. The tray in the hands of the priest began to tremble. The water in it spilled and the boys who had sneaked up to see the bull at close quarters, decided that they should save themselves from the bull's rearing and sought to hide themselves in the crowd. The Patil's beloved stay-at-home son-in-law wondered what would happen if the animal broke loose and went for the Patil.

Guna Gurav was staring at the bull and was hurrying to complete his task. The Patil was looking at him with a fixed gaze and a fear-desiccated face. The Mahars bearing the sword and the axe were staring at the Patil's cane and some people were looking at the expanse of Deva's chest and simultaneously at the bull's dread mien; others were simply avoiding the bull's eyes.

Gurav signalled to the Patil. The Patil said something inside his mouth and asked Deva: 'How much?'

'Fifty,' said Deva.

'If the bull runs off…' Kulkarni asked.

'Time walks in fear of me. This Mahar's head will take the beating. But this head is not made of manure. Go on. Hit it.'

'Shall I?'

Deva swelled up his chest and gave permission.

With the sword in one hand and the stick in the other, the Patil stood up in the purified space. The sword- and axe-bearing Mahars were on the alert. The basket came down from the head to the stomach and the fourth Mahar spread his dhotar in front of him.

The Patil, forcing his hand to remain steady, put the stick on the bull's ear. 'Hold tight,' Deva told his companions. The touch of the stick let loose a storm of movement in the animal's muscles. The crowd was as still as a picture.

When the stick was removed, the sword came down and sliced off the animal's ear and rose again. The ear went into the dhotar's folds. Blood spurted into the basket. The animal bucked as if electrified.

The whole crowd responded. That bucking reduced the Patil's courage to tatters. The crowd was drenched in fear. Even the toughest were quaking.

With his lids locked laterally, the Patil stared at the terrifying beast as he placed his stick on the second ear. And without damaging the skull in any way, the axe rose and fell and sliced off the second ear. Maddened by pain, the bull gathered all his strength to break free. The four lost control and the beast began to drag them along. But even as the crowd screamed, Deva got control of it again and pulled it back into the enclosure. The Patil recovered a little. The crowd gathered around the beast again as people calmed down and returned to their original places.

Everyone was looking at the Patil as he placed his cane on the animal's tail. The stick moved. The sword flashed down and rose again, cutting off the tail. The bull pulled free. The crowd immediately gave way. The Patil was left alone and at a loss.

The young men accompanying the Patil fled into the crowd. Another developed a spontaneous insane courage. He ran at the animal with a spear in his hands. Behind him, Rabu Chamaar screamed his heart out: 'Hey Paatla… get out of the way.' But the Patil did not move. The spear hit the bull where it should not have. And that caused the bull to break all bounds and it began to run and all hell broke loose.

'They'll die, those pimps…' said an old man in a rage so violent, his hair stood all over his body.

'There are four of them!' the arrogant young man retorted.

'Arre, he's fallen, he's fallen!' The bull, in agony from the wound in its genitals, was now cowering. It raised its hind leg and kicked out in Hari's general direction. Hari jumped forward and got hold of it again. In their fear, everyone was shouting confused directions. The noise stiffened the animal's resolve. It lashed out, and its side caught Hari and he slipped and fell. The bull thundered off, dragging him along as it went.

'Arre, Devoo, hey Deva, get him up. Stop the bull,' everyone was screaming. In the meanwhile, Hari was being dragged along as the bull ran, free of all control. Both Deva and Shiva were trying to stop it but they could only run alongside the beast. They could not stop it. Hari was desperately trying to keep his limbs from under the hooves. But the bull was not to be stopped nor would it let him get up again. He could not get his hand loose either. Behind him, the man carrying the flowers threw the bundles away and was trying to get Hari to listen to him. But Hari was too busy trying to free his hand and stay out of the bull's way. Everyone was trying their best with directions and gestures and signals. The bakulawala would not set his basket down and clung to it as if it were a talisman against ghosts.

And the bull kept on dragging Hari.

Kisan was completely out of it. He could not think, he could not figure out how to stop the animal, what to do, nothing occurred to him. He just ran with the bull, ran without tiring.

'Shiva, use your body to stop it,' Deva was holding

on the horns. He was using his shoulders and with the other hand he was pushing the bull towards Shiva. Shiva was running, running with the animal, trying to change its trajectory. The bull turned. Taking hold of the rope in Hari's hand, Deva shouted, 'Let go.'

'Dead, he's gone...' the basket case let out a wail. Deva turned back. The bull had one hoof on Hari's wrist. The cord had come loose from his hand.

'Give it here, Deva.' With the cord disentangled, Hari leaped up like a snake rearing, his body bloodied, and began to run to get hold of the rope. He bent down to get hold of it but it kept moving out of his reach, and each time he would bend down and grab at it and miss... then he ran and bent over and fell and did not rise again.

The ground was slaking its thirst with the blood that burst like fountains from the bull's ears. The flowers were still being drenched in blood. The wounds were like constant prods, spurring the animal to action. The alcohol sent madness spinning through its blood vessels and Deva would now have to take his life into his own hands to stop it.

Now the Patil was back on his horse, striking an arrogant pose. His sword beat upon the air, slicing it, staying it, holding it still. He came forward a few steps, then took a huge turn and his unsheathed sword went back to its original spot. Now his face was much less stern.

Hari was picked up and brought to him.

'Arre, not there...'

Hari, who had brought the bull to the temple, could not be taken into it. He was carried to the Maharwada.

The bull's speed increased. Fire was racing through its

body. Inside its brain, the desire to plunge its burning body into water began to grow. And so it turned towards the well in the neighbouring field. Seeing the direction the bull had taken, the people from the neighbouring village began to play the daf to provoke it, to anger it. And so it forced its way into the neighbouring village and began to head towards Rakhma Patil.

Now everyone, including Deva, had got the measure of the beast. And so the roar of people's shouting began to resound there. Hearing the noise and confusion, whatever little brain was left inside the bull's head began to melt and run out of him with his sweat. He began to cross the boundary. He was now eager to knock Shiva and Deva, the two obstacles in his path, out of his way. He rocked his body and shook it. He bucked his head. Seeing this, Kisan was terrified. The strength in his arms and thighs waned.

'Here he is,' from the neighbouring fields, the people began to warn each other.

'Carefully!' the armed men from the neighbouring village stepped forward. Right in front, the shining sword of Rakhma Patil glittered.

Last year, the same thing had happened. The enraged bull had taken four Mahars down in this very manner and according to tradition, Rakhma Patil had claimed the bull and the sacrifice, hitting it on its forehead and symbolically shaming the Mahars too.

'Gone away,' Deva's folks cried out in defeat.

If he had not been moved by the fear of death, perhaps it was the fear of disgrace that made Deva stick his hand into the beast's mouth and pull him back. Rakhma Patil's attack went empty handed.

The bull's cheek split right up to its ears. Blood flowed freely. Now there was no resistance in its body. Its limbs were limp. It was desperate with pain. It was now in Deva's complete control. Shiva brought it back to the boundary of the village. The Patil looked at them now. As he watched Deva, it seemed as if Yamraj himself was approaching. His blood-stained face and victorious eyes frightened the Patil.

His heart began to thunder and his hackles rose. He made his face expressionless. He approached upon his shrivelled legs. He inflated his chest. He held his head high. Not even looking at Deva, not even by mistake, in high style, he placed his stick on the animal and the sword came down as a bolt of lightning and then rose with as much speed. The powerful head of the bull fell upon the ground. The Patil held the sword in the stream of blood. The apta leaves were drenched in blood. The Patil now mounted his dwarf steed in high style and rode away, into the darkness, rode away home.

In the door of his home, he stopped to strike a pose, the pose of a man who has encountered death and fought it and returned. And his wife came out with an aarti thali and saluted his great victory.

Meanwhile the villagers began to take away the blood-wet apta leaves, now true gold. The Mahars buried the bull's head near the gate and brought the rest of the carcass into the Maharwada.

Deva's wife laughed and wiped away her tears as she emerged from the terror of what had seemed like imminent widowhood, and she turned in all four directions and made salutations to the elements in praise of his victory.

Monkey

BAPU PEHELWAN WAS as huge and cruel as a bear but his brain was the size of an ant's. This half-uncivilized and somewhat wild man, whose footwear weighed a kilo or a kilo-and-a-half, was pacing about as restlessly as an animal trapped in a cage, an axe over his shoulder. From time to time, he would look at the village with longing; and the very next moment, with an equal rage, he would turn his back on it. His grip on the axe would tighten. And in anger, he would curse his wife.

Over the past two days, his naïve, blind, immature mind had been filled with lust for Sakhu; that he should feel this made him angry and this would initiate a battle between the desire to deceive and the desire to keep his promises. He was a buffalo tormented by a horsefly.

The next day there was a prestigious wrestling match at the jatra; at this match, he would have a chance to win back his lost pride. A Koli pehelwan from his in-laws' village had defeated him and pinned him to the ground. That it should have been someone of a lower caste and the man should have come from that particular area made it worse. He had made a promise that he would defeat not just that pehelwan but three others as well. In order to keep his promise and win the competition, he had left his beautiful young wife and had exiled himself from his own home, living in a hut in the fields as if he were cattle. He had made a vow of celibacy, and was keeping his word with great difficulty. He had pawned his land and spent the money as if it were water, and was eating khuraak* every day. He exercised until the sweat poured off him and wet the ground. He practised wrestling by the hour; both his strength and his hope of winning were increasing every day.

But now that the competition was close, his mind was playing tricks on him. After the last defeat, he and his mother had decided that his wife was the enemy—but memories of Sakhu now tormented him. So that these should not return, and in so returning, ruin his vow of celibacy, he prayed to both Bajrangbali** and Vetaal†.

But still Sakhu would not budge from her tantalizing position in his head. He was so enraged by this that he even considered murdering her and being done with it. And in the same moment, he would wish she would come to him in the farm and that thought would terrify him. This was why his raging, lustful eyes kept turning to the village to catch a glimpse of her. His entire body, mind and spirit seemed to be calling out to her. But jealousy, the challenge he had issued and fear of his mother held him in check.

---

*Khuraak is a mixture of dry fruits, dates and jaggery that is believed to build strength.

**Bajrangbali is the God of the Wrestling Pit and is also celibate.

†A vetaal is a ghost-like figure which haunts crematoria.

And even as he was struggling with the twin demons of lust and rage, he spied Sakhu on her way to the field. Her body was slim and the colour of copper; her hair was long and soft. She was carrying a basket of food on her head. The sight of her was enough to make him turn his back on her and run into the hut in rage and fear. Inside the hut, the sight of the bed made him want to throw down the axe he had raised to his shoulders and run back out to see her. (He generally stationed the axe next to the door, just in case someone from his in-laws' decided to pay him a night visit.) Now he set it down and maddened by lust, he began to drink in the vision of Sakhu approaching. That she was walking slowly made him angry. He wanted to drag her to him.

Sakhu too had been longing to see her husband after six months of separation. She had felt it would afford her as much pleasure as seeing a peacock. Then she suddenly found the opportunity. Her mother-in-law had left in the morning, to see the bhagat* and even when it was time to take Bapu his meal, the old woman had not returned. And although she had been strictly forbidden from seeing her husband since this might cause him to break his vow, the need to see him had been so strong that she had ignored her terrifying mother-in-law's proscription and had set off for the hut in the fields.

But when she saw her husband, his body as powerful and frightful as that of a demon, her desire came to an abrupt end. Fear made her limp. She knew she had broken the ban and was afraid that he would attack her like an

---

*A bhagat, in this context, is a priest who deals in occult practices.

enraged bull and then her mother-in-law would burn her with live coal and would keep her hungry and all this made her want to turn back. And yet there was no way she could do this either. She knew that if she went back, she would be punished. And so she decided that she might as well see her husband, but her feet would not move and she could only inch forward.

Seeing her pace decrease, the fire went from his heels to his head. In order to urge her to come faster, he roared, 'Sakhé!'

Her husband's roar encouraged her and she came swiftly up to him, expecting a blow. But he only looked at her face. 'Why so late?'

Instead of answering, she lowered her head. Seeing her fear, her vulnerability and the fact that she was on the verge of tears, his lust transmuted into rage and he shouted, 'What is it?'

Sure that he was going to hit her, she took two steps back. And then he leapt upon her and pulled her to his body. That caused the basket she was carrying on her head to fall over and the bowl of vegetables she was carrying over-turned, spilling its contents over her shoulders.

As soon as she realized that her husband was not going to beat her for disobeying orders, she said in a soft voice, 'Let me go. Have something to eat. You must be hungry. Tomorrow is the jatra…'

'The jatra tomorrow…' he let go of her. She went into the hut immediately and putting the basket down, she began to sweep with a coir broom. She took the bedding from the cot and folded it and tidied up. Then she carried the basket into the living room and just as she got here, he pounced on her again, dragging her to him.

'Let me go. Tomorrow is your wrestling match.'

'I won't.'

'Then come home tonight…'

'What? You think I'm frightened of the old lady?' he snarled and flung her away from him as if she were a kitten. She tried to rise but before she could get to her feet, he had her by the hair and was dragging her up to press her against his body; he did not let her go until the pressure that had been built up in his body was released. When he realized that he had now broken his vow to remain celibate, rage exploded in his heart. Gathering all his strength and willpower once again, he threw her away from him. This time when she fell, she hit the bamboo shutters with great force. Her nose began to bleed and her lips and face began to swell up.

That her nose was bleeding and her face was swollen did not bother him. On the contrary, his fear of his mother and his shame at having broken his vow of celibacy made him uncontrollably angry for he held her responsible for what had happened. The hatred he felt for her made him want to see her dead. Now he was so frightened of his mother coming back that the desire to crack her head open as one might break a coconut spread through his blood like a drug. He went forward to kill her.

But the sight of the rising slopes of her chest and the slenderness of her waist turned his murderous rage into a cruel lust. The hands that had wanted to pick her up and slam her on the ground now scooped her up and as he was walking to the bed in the corner, his mother appeared in the doorway, standing there with a bundle of food tied up on her head; and seeing the scene in the hut, in rage and in sorrow, she screamed in a voice loud enough to pierce the eardrums—'You stinking corpse, put her down, drop her, I say. Tomorrow is the wrestling match and today you think of this outrage, you rotter. What did you think you were doing with her? Are you going to get your honour back by picking up this prostitute as if she were a child? God, God above, you stupid animal, you beast, if this is what you wanted to do, why did you put me to so much expense? For you, I pawned our land. And I stuffed all that money into your stomach. Was it for this? Set her down now, drop that slut.'

The old lady was out of control. Her hands were itching to grab Sakhu by the throat and kill her. The terrible accusation froze him to the spot. He continued to stand there, holding Sakhu in his arms, staring at his mother, dumb, an idiot. Sakhu, still in his arms, was frightened almost to death.

'You buffalo, put her down. Grind her in the mud. I tell you, stamp on her, crush her,' the old lady's face was red with anger. Her eyes, terrifying now, seemed transfixed on the figure of Sakhu. She wanted to snap her in two, to eat her alive, to crunch her up as one might a cucumber. She wanted to go forward, she was fighting the urge for she was also aware that she had, on her head, the makings of a spell from the bhagat and if it were set down betimes, that too would be wasted.

His mother's words had the effect of camphor-soaked cotton touched by fire—they burned away in minutes what little brain he had.

'Bullock...' His stone-like immobility enraged her so much that she ran forward, her anger now completely erasing all awareness of the bhagat's magic material that she was carrying on her head. When she got near him, she hit him around the head and dragging Sakhu from his arms, let her fall to the ground. Then she raised a leg to kick her. That finally upset the bundle that she had been carrying and it fell on Sakhu's chest. Seeing the bundle fall broke her heart. Her eyes filled with tears. Without even knowing it, she drew back the foot she had extended, sat down and let loose a wail of extreme sorrow and anger. 'The worst has happened, you stupid beast, you animal, this is a calamity… The game is over now… Hundreds of rupees wasted…'

She was slapping her face with both hands; then she began to slap her breast and her stomach. Like someone mad, she sobbed and wept and banged her head upon the ground. Watching his mother like this made him lose all power of speech. He simply stood still and looked at the old lady, and from time to time, over to where Sakhu lay unconscious, with the bundle still lying on top of her.

Slowly a way of calming the old lady came into his head. He fell upon the recumbent form of Sakhu. As he beat her, words came back to him, came back with each blow. 'Slut, tell me why you came here?'

But how could she answer the question? The blind worship a Hindu woman offers her husband, the tug of a new attraction had brought her there. She had been curious about how he would now look after all the pains he had endured, and it was this dangerous curiosity that had lured her there. How could she talk of these hopes and fears as she lay unconscious? And even had she been conscious, how could she, a respectable girl, speak as she took such a beating?

But he kept hitting her and asking the same question. Now the old lady's tears were abating. As she watched her son beating his wife, she said, 'Arre animal, blockhead, ask me why she came. She wanted you to lose tomorrow. She wanted to destroy your vow of celibacy. Rambha* was here to make sure those Mahar Kolis win tomorrow. Let her go. It's done. It's over.'

'Aah?' Hearing the old lady's venomous explanation, his mind, not much better than a monkey's, was completely overpowered by his rage. He began to throw Sakhu here and there, as a dog might throw a rat. Her body went limp, blood spurted from many places, it covered her everywhere but the sight of it only inflamed him further. His eyes now sought the axe by the door, he wanted to finish her off. The old lady saw this murderous intent and now she spoke lovingly:

'Go my son, go have a bath. If it be your destiny, Lord Maruti will stand by your side. The sin was this prostitute's. Go pray. Beg forgiveness of God and let us see...'

And like a monkey trained to obey, that huge wrestler went for a dip in the pond, immersed himself and came back up.

'Take that bundle, sprinkle water over it, purify it. Burn camphor and incense, and wave them over it. Tomorrow put on a fresh langot and a new dhotar. Tie that gandha dor** around your neck and break a coconut.

---

*Rambha is an apsara, often used by the Gods to distract a man whose penances are beginning to disrupt the order of things.

**A string dipped in sandalwood paste and worn as a talisman against evil or the evil eye.

I've spent a hundred rupees. God will not let that go in vain. Come home. Let her remain. Tomorrow, we'd better beware of those people. Come.'

Leaving innocent Sakhu lying there, he walked after his mother in wet clothes. His mother seemed to him like a warrior and he, nothing more than a lamb.

The old lady walked ahead. She was depressed at the thought that Sakhu's touch had vitiated everything: the gandha dor, the langot, the dhotar were all unclean. But she did not want her son to feel the same way, so in order to give him some hope, she said: 'I got up in the morning and went to meet the bhagat who lives on the hill. I spent a hundred rupees on all this. That prostitute saw I was not at home and decided to take the chance. But what of it? This langot will make sure you win. You will give it your all, won't you?'

He nodded like a little child. The old lady grew sad and wiped her eyes.

The next day, in front of thousands, he fought again and once again he was pinned to the ground. Once again, he had to bow his head in defeat and leave the stage and so he began to beat Sakhu again, saying, 'You lost the match for me.' He sought to break her. Sakhu suffered fractures and was confined to bed. His mother and he were the laughingstock of ten villages. And angry and ashamed, she now was urging her son to murder the victor.

And her son, trained monkey that he was, began to sharpen his axe…

Competition

'BEGGAR, SCAVENGER, WILL you eat from my hand and then yell at me? You go to that prostitute to eat, give her money and ruin me! Arre, Baamna*, I am the wife of Shiva Pehelwan, you won't get away with this...'

Enraged, Yamuna, the old woman who sold bananas, was cursing and screaming at Pratap Pande, a Brahmin from Uttar Pradesh. As she shouted, her gaze, rich with the fire of her rage, flicked from the addiction-riddled and vice-raddled body of Pratap Pande, to the beautiful body of Chandra, the young woman who was sitting beside her.

This was actually Yamuna's nephew's wife, who had her plump and shapely back to Yamuna. She was talking to her clients, entertaining them with coquettish movements of the head and captivating them with her laughter. One of these men was Pratap Pande and now he looked to the young woman for some help with pitiable eyes.

But that beautiful woman was ignoring him totally and laughing with everyone else; and that caused his ganja-inflamed heart to burn with rage. What with

---

*In this case, a pejorative use of Brahmin. I have heard it used affectionately as well, but between Brahmins.

Chandra ignoring him and the old lady castigating him, screaming at him with no self-control, the debt-ridden Brahmin found himself asking, 'What money are you talking about?'

'Your father's!'

The pain she had felt on reading her son's aching letters, the shame of losing out to the competition, made her gall rise and she flung herself on Pande like a tiger. Wherever she could lay her hands, whether on cloth or on skin, she rained her blows. His clothes began to tear under her onslaught. While watching him being shamed, not one of his fellowmen from his village came to his aid, neither did the Ahirs and Kunbis and this made him so angry at the disrespect that he began to abuse in his arrogant Uttar Pradeshi dialect.

He tried to get hold of the old woman's neck to push her to the ground, the better to throttle her—'Shameless hag, trying to beat me!'

This made the old lady, her business totally destroyed by her daughter-in-law's beauty, only try all the harder. She began to chase him as he ran, and he started to hop about here and there like a chicken, trying simultaneously to get away and to land a few himself. It was Chandra who warned him, 'Pandya, keep your hands down.'

Almost in tears out of the disrespect and the shame, poor, thin Pande dropped his hands and looking at Chandra, said with tears in his voice: 'Look at your mother-in-law, she beats Brahmins. Has she any shame or what?'

Chandra made no reply. She knew what a unique woman Yamuna was, how wide and expansive her heart.

She knew the reasons for the old lady's sorrow, but she could do nothing to dispel it, for she knew that to do so would destroy her. And so she said nothing and became grave.

That Chandra should intervene in this manner and that Pande should listen to her inflamed the old lady further. Now she turned on Chandra and began to abuse her. Seeing that Yamuna's attention had been diverted, Pratap Pande tried to slip away into the crowd but the old lady ran after him and caught him. Watching all this running and romping, the assembled crowd began to laugh and hearing the vindictive and disrespectful sound of that laughter, the proud old lady wanted to weep but she suppressed her tears and said, 'Dog, will you eat my food and then bark at me? Will you chase me to beat me? I've been observing the change in your behaviour ever since you started listening to that prostitute. No one gives me credit, when I go to ask they refuse, they don't speak kindly to me. They don't even look out for me, not even by mistake. Why have you ruined me like this? Was it my fault that I felt some affection for you? Don't I have a stomach? Only that slut has one, right? You go and bow and scrape in front of her. But remember this: she's the daughter-in-law of Bhosales, a kingly family. She's not one of your toss-skirts...' But as her throat was choked with tears, she could not say what was in her heart.

Out of Chandra's heart rose the thought, '...I am the daughter-in-law of a royal family and I behave like a prostitute for my husband...' and in a second, her cheerful face went sad and serious. The people around her who had enjoyed her wise-cracking wondered what had happened. Kisan felt that the old woman had to be driven away, whatever it took. Her curses and abuses had made Chandra withdraw and shrivel. As long as the old woman was around, Chandra would not be his. He decided he would ruin the old woman. 'That poor woman,' thought Chandra, 'she's a good thing; they shouldn't treat her like this...'

The cruelty and the distant behaviour of the workers whom the old lady had treated as her own was something she could not bear and she burst into a loud ululation. The people around her began to mumble and murmur: How could this wise, composed old lady suddenly go mad? Some people began to feel pain in their hearts. Some were simply baffled. Seeing the old lady's helplessness, Pratap Pande was flummoxed. He began to feel that he must have done something evil. His ganja-dulled and anti-social heart tore open and as light comes streaming through a window that has just been broken, his ganja-fogged eyes could now see the past and the old lady's abundant loving-kindness.

For over the last fifteen years, Yamuna had been selling bananas in front of the factory. In those fifteen years, she had never offended anyone in speech, never argued over credit. She behaved as a mother might with everyone, never forgetting for a moment that she herself was a mother. This magnificent maternal spirit had been evident in everything she said, in everything she did, in every second of her time there. She had made every attempt to reform Pratap. When he had been hungry and had had no money for food, she had taken out some rupees and given them to him without him even asking. She had devised several ways and means to rid him of his debts and his worries. Had he followed her suggestions, his life would have been vastly improved. This wonderful woman, who had cared for all the grieving and the hopeless, had suddenly changed dramatically in the last three or four months into a horrible harridan. And the reason was the beautiful Chandra.

It was she who had set Chandra up to work there. She told every single person she knew that Chandra was her nephew's wife, a daughter-in-law to her. And so the immoral and the lustful were forewarned and spoke to Chandra as they ought rather than as they wanted. Not too many bought from her as they feared the old lady's suspicion. But then unhappy Chandra also did not so much as look at her customers. It was as if speaking to them was an effort that cost her much. When she accepted money or gave the change, her melancholic face would brighten up for a bit. If someone's gaze fell upon her beautiful body, she reacted as a sparrow caught in a fire might. She would rush to cover herself up. In fear and shame, she would pull her pallu from her forehead right down to her nose. Seeing such discomfiture, the voyeur would be embarrassed; and because of this some well-behaved workers would never buy from her.

But in just one month, the mild, melancholic Chandra had changed completely. Her head was up, her gaze became bold, the pallu of her sari only got to her head to slip back to her blouse and if it fell off her breast, she didn't bother too much. Her hair took on a new look and her soft full lips took on the rich red of the paan she now chewed. She began to walk with such enjoyment and to laugh too—and wore such attractive blouses and saris that the people flocked to her. The young men now vied with each other to make a conquest of her; and she gave each one separate and individual cause for hope. If anyone were to ask the reason for this miraculous transformation, the reply would be: 'My husband's flat on his back.'

Each one made what he wanted of this answer; and each became Chandra's customer in the hope of acquiring her. Which meant the old lady's basket went untouched.

Yamuna could only stare in astonishment at Chandra. She tried to control Chandra, who seemed to her like a calf that has become intoxicated, but the young woman paid not the slightest heed. She continued to behave like a streetwalker. The old lady began to fight with her. For, after much thought, Yamuna had figured out what Chandra was up to. She surmised that Chandra had decided to get rid of her and so the old lady in her turn had decided to get Chandra out of there with a constant barrage of abuse. Every day, she picked a fight with Chandra. Thinking about all this, Pratap Pande said to the old lady, 'Look, Auntie, I will give you all your money when I get my pay. I won't keep anything back. Let me go now.' Pratap's eyes were filled with tears.

His pitiful condition did not soften the old lady. She reached for a hank of his hair and said, 'You thief, you'll give me my money? A fork-tongued snake would be better than you. No, I'm going to get you by the hair and drag you to the manager. Only then will I get some peace.'

She made a lunge for his head again but now the crowd turned against her and began to shout as if in one voice, 'Old hag, let him go.'

'Why?' she asked, turning on them. But there was no force to her words.

'He'll pay you...and we won't let you go to the manager...will you ruin him forever?' the crowd demanded.

The old lady retreated. Tears began to flow from her eyes. How could these people turn against her because of one woman? Did none of them remember her kindness, the affection she had showered on them? The pain of these insults filled her mouth with ashes. She let Pratap go with a, 'Go on then, Baba...'

She could say nothing further.

She fell to weeping for a while and then in a mournful tone, said: 'Arre, why are you burying me before I am dead? Why are you beating a corpse? Oh big men, you've been letting that prostitute pour poison into your ears— and so you treat someone who was like your mother at one time as you would a snake; you look at her as if she's a scorpion. Why do you treat me as if I am your enemy?'

She began to sob. At her heart-rending words, the crowd began to be moved. Some of them simply slipped away while others stayed on to talk about this.

The old lady's weeping stopped. Her face had become extraordinarily savage. Her eyes were aflame. She was staring fixedly at the factory. And as she stared, she rose, her pose that of a fighter, and ran to attack her terrified daughter-in-law. Someone raised an alarm—'The old woman has run mad.'

Yamuna planted herself in front of Chandra and demanded, 'Are you satisfied? Did you get what you want? These people who have known me for years think

I am mad. *I* am mad? *I* am disturbed? *My* affection is mad?'

Chandra could not look at her. She had bowed her head. She curled into a ball, out of fear. Kisan, who would give his life for Chandra, could not bear to see her in this state. He got to his feet and shouted, 'Ay mad woman, get out of here! Are you going or do I have to hit you?'

'I am mad, am I?'

'You've decided to get rid of her. Your constant bickering gives her no peace. Remember this: if you say anything to her now, I'm going to break your legs…'

'You will break my legs? Shiva's mother's legs? If he hears of this, he'll break you like an onion.'

'So bring him here then.' He had long decided that Yamuna was the reason why Chandra had not let herself be drawn to him; she respected the old lady too much. So he, and all the others who were mad about Chandra, had also long sought a way to get rid of Yamuna. Being kept away from Chandra set his heart afire. And with all this accumulated spite, he shouted: 'If I see you here tomorrow…'

'What will you do?'

'I'll give you such a beating…'

And with this he turned to attack the old woman. In that moment, sensing what he was about to do, Chandra caught hold of his arm to hold him back. The touch of her hand cooled his ire but he did not want her to stop touching him and so he pretended to be angrier still and started to shout. And seeing the pleasure that he derived from Chandra's touch, two or three others who were also attracted to her, got jealous and began to fight with the old lady; and seeing these ignoble men's roughness, Chandra began to feel terrible, as if her very guts were being ripped out. She begged each one of them to stop. She kept pulling Kisan back. But none of them listened to her. None of them was willing to retreat. And the old lady turned red as a flame at the sight of such ingratitude but she could not say anything. She was already aware that it was a mistake to fight with clients. And so to Chandra, she said, 'Look, look, how a child from the dancing-and-singing community takes the hand of any man from any caste. You sinner, you will destroy all these men. For the love of money, do not consign all these families to hell like this. That boy will also be consumed by your sins.'

Hearing the old lady's mad, fiery speech, Chandra let go of Kisan's hand. She felt she might have made a mistake; she was not sure how much Kisan loved her. If she had not had his support, she would not have been able to support her husband; and it was this knowledge that tormented her. In the last two years, she had wanted to accept him, wanted it with all the lust of her young body, but she could not do so.

The grateful eyes of her sick husband, his words that offered her worship for all the things she did for him and his smile, his welcoming smile that greeted her every day, and all the admiration he had expressed since his return from Mumbai, all this took priority and she began to feel as if she were a sinner. To calm her mind, she would dedicate herself to saving him with even greater intensity. That his tuberculosis should be defeated was her goal. To attain this, she needed more money; to get more money she had forced herself to become uninhibited; she had tried to please the male clients with her ploys and artifices. She would take what she was given and then, at the right moment, she would disappear. They would wait eagerly for her, their craving unfulfilled. This meant she earned a lot more; but none of it gave her any peace.

For she knew she was playing a dangerous game. As a woman, she was well aware that Kisan and the others were not going to bear this forever and she did not have the strength to keep up the farce much longer. She knew that she would have to give herself to one of them. Or she would end up with the reputation of a woman who took money and did not deliver and no one would let her sit in front of the factory. Some hothead might decide to shame her in front of everyone or even take her life; and then what would happen to her husband? What would happen to her? She wished now that she had not acted in this way, blindly, just for the money. The old lady's reputation would have been intact; and this conflagration would not have erupted.

As these thoughts occurred to her, she felt a great rage against herself, her husband and all those who were mad about her youth and beauty. She turned this rage on the old woman in front of her and said: 'Look, don't you get after me. If you keep on doing this, I'll take opium and kill myself. Or I'll just get hold of the next fellow who comes along and go to Hell. Got it? I beg of you. And if you flap your lips again, you'll get your answer with chappals...'

'Why wait? Hit me now. Pay me back right now for all that I have done for you...' Yamuna shouted and attacked her again. But Chandra, who already felt that she had overstepped the limits, had drooped. Her body had no strength left in it. Uncontrollable now, the old lady fell upon Chandra.

If shame made Chandra droop, then rage at this made her rise again. She bent down to take off her slippers to belabour the old lady with them. This gave the old lady the chance to get her by the hair and yank her down. Chandra's desire for revenge ran out of her with her strength. Maddened by pain, she lay as she had fallen and howled. Hearing this, Kisan renewed his attack on the old lady. He was fighting with her while the others were laying lascivious hands on Chandra, hands that sought to tease and hurt under the pretext of helping her up.

'Go away, animals! Do you have mothers and sisters? Is this any way to behave?' Tears were pouring from her eyes.

'Who hurt you, Chandra?' Kisan let go of the old woman to go to her aid.

'Look at this...' she was about to pull her sari pallu aside to show him where she had been hurt when she realized what an error her pain and rage had brought her to. Her head went down and she began to sob. The old lady melted. She came forward to hug Chandra, when Kisan, who had grown angry with his friends, left them and confronted her: 'Get away, hag...'

Chandra raised her head to look; and in order not to lose her client, she took out the rage she was feeling against them on the old woman: 'From now on, you are no longer my mother-in-law. You're dead for me. See if I ever call you mother-in-law again. Say another word to me and see what happens.'

'Like that, is it?'

'That is how it is. For so long, I've been burning up my life, camphor for that corpse; not any more. I won't poison him either. I'll keep him alive. If you don't like my behaviour, then look after him yourself. Tie him to your neck and dance. If I feel like it, I will have one man. Or ten.'

'Have you stooped so low?'

'Lower.'

'Then I too will stoop to your depths. If he dies, let him. I don't care. Go threaten his parents.'

'His parents are your brother-in-law and sister-in-law. They're safe and sound in the village. They wail and weep, "He's our son, he's our son", but they've dumped this dead body on me. And if something happens to me, they'll toss me out and marry that corpse off again.'

'Slut, don't talk like that. Worms will crawl out of your mouth. Will you raise a hand against your mother-in-law?'

'I have not so far. But I will. I will do as I please. If you can't bear to watch, pluck out your eyes. Or move on and start again elsewhere.'

'You're puffed up because you have all these men around you. But I am also Shiva's mother. He won't rest until he's taught you a lesson.'

'Tell him what you want. I will care for him as long as I can and have the strength. If I succeed, well and good. If not, I'll find myself another.'

'I can see that.'

'Keep it up. Wait until tomorrow. Then you'll really see something.'

Hearing her words, Kisan was delighted. Now he had no doubt that Chandra was going to be his. And Chandra too, ignoring her mother-in-law, set her hair in order and said to him, 'Come and get it, Kisanrao,' and gave him paan.

'Try and be sensible. I am your mother-in-law…'

'Oh yes, like a mother-in-law!'

'Remember all that was done for you. How well you have repaid your obligations. Your husband was dying of hunger. And I, like a mad woman, took pity on you. If I had known that you would repay me with such selfishness, would I have brought you here and set you up right next to me? God, my God…How am I to help my poor child, Shiva? Letter after letter comes from him…' And tears poured from the old woman's eyes. 'Chandra, this is not how you should have behaved…'

'I want to keep my husband alive,' Chandra replied immediately.

'And I want my poor Shiva to settle down and be happy. Chandra, my daughter-in-law is far better than you…' and the old lady left.

The old lady's last line shocked Chandra. The news of the arrival of the old lady's daughter-in-law frightened her and in order to rid her mind of the fear, she opened her paan packet and called out to a worker who had been eyeing her body with evil intent. 'Arre masthur*, come on over…'

'What are you calling him for?' Kisan was still angry with her. And now that he felt Chandra was going to be his, he wanted nothing to do with any of his other friends. 'Why are you calling him over?'

---

*'Masthur' derives from the English 'master' but has specific resonances here of affection and familiarity, and so I have retained it unchanged.

'I have to do business, don't I?'

'What need when I am here?'

'How many bunches of bananas will you eat every day?' she asked and laughed immoderately.

And finding no trace of softness anywhere, in her voice or in her laughter, he stared at her. Now that the old lady had gone, her zest had increased. She was calling out to everyone she could see. Her words were sleazy. Her jokes were lewd. She did not think about this at all. And so a crowd began to gather around her again. Her sales were brisk. Kisan did not like her behaviour but because he wanted her so badly, he bore it all day and so two days fled like birds to the East.

And Chandra's heart began to beat in fear. For the men around her were no longer behaving well; they were now ridiculing her. They were using every opportunity to lay hands on her. All those she had tantalized were now demanding their pound of flesh. Only Kisan was silent. From time to time, he intervened. He would sit by her for a while and then go away. That frightened her even more but she could not hold him there. If she did, she would lose her independence. And since he was not of her caste, this seemed to her to be a sin. But having him nearby made her happy. Once they were alone for a moment, she said:

'Why isn't the old lady coming back?'

'Good she's gone, that unmitigated ringworm!'

'Don't say that. She's good at heart. She has a son and is in great need because of him. And I've gone and ruined the poor thing. She even took a loan to set me up here. That's why she was angry, and went roaring about like a tiger. And if she brings her daughter-in-law here to get even with me…'

'What will happen?' Kisan asked.

Afraid that the men who had been attracted by her beauty would simply forsake her for someone who was more beautiful, she said: 'It will be a disaster for me.'

'Is she prettier than you?' The question hurt her. She began to doubt Kisan, to dislike him.

'Yes. What will I do if she comes here?'

'I'm here for you, Chandra. Now I don't want to wait. I'll give you whatever you ask for, I'll out it all in your name: my provident fund, my salary, my home, my land, everything. You'll be a queen.'

This pretty speech did not fill her heart with happiness. Instead it made it thump with rage. But she kept control of her voice and said with feigned ignorance, 'Kisanrao, what's your caste?'

This disingenuous and deliberately offensive question wounded him and he said, 'Chandra, you should not have asked me like that. If you wanted to ask such a question, you should not have taken what I gave. You should not have made promises on every occasion. I have seen your eyes full of desire so many times. I have listened to your words. Which is why I held myself in patience. I did not see you as a prostitute; I know you aren't one, though I have to say that you behave like one. And if your fate determines that such a time should come in your life, instead of giving in to all comers, call me.'

And he rose abruptly and left, and just at that moment the siren announcing the end of the shift went off and a great crowd of workers emerged from the factory.

'Aaho Kisanrao,' she longed to call out to him, the constant bedfellow of her dreams. But the words would not emerge from her mouth. And even if they had, Kisan who had got lost in the crowd, would not have heard them.

Until the last worker left, she was busy selling, but that line of his—*You may not be a prostitute but you act like one*—blared in her ears. It kept her mind in turmoil. For she had kept him on a string for a long time, fooling him and herself too. For her young body and her mind had been calling out to him, every night, and this had enslaved her, she knew this well.

When most of the workers had gone away, she ignored the one or two who were still hanging around her and went home sadly.

The next day, when she arrived she saw the old woman and her willpower collapsed entirely. For to the surprise of the entire factory, the old lady was sitting there with a young and gorgeous girl by her side. Yamuna was calling out to everyone she knew. She knew almost every worker, and one by one, she was calling them over and muttering into their ears. And each man whose ear was being bent by the old woman was being subjected to some astonishing coquetry by the young woman. The old woman was already selling her wares. Each customer who went to Yamuna left Chandra with a feeling of defeat and anger. She wanted to go up to the old woman and demand an explanation but she did not get up from her place. Not one of her usual customers came to her that day. All of them gathered around the new arrival. Kisan cast a single glance at her and went into the factory. She felt glad that he had not stopped near the new woman but this was tempered by the sadness that he did not stop and talk to her either. She sat there and waited. Finally some people did come and buy from her.

One of those who had managed to lay hands on her the day before asked, 'Chandra, do you know her?'

'Yes.'

'She's a prostitute. Now you will have to become like her as well,' he taunted and looked at her, waiting for an answer. She was so angry, she wanted to slap him but she said nothing. Not a word came out of her lips. He saw that she was not going to reply and he went off. And so Chandra, controlling her tears, went to her mother-in-law and said to her in a soft voice:

'...Now I will have to become a prostitute like this girl, and you will have to look after my basket. I am a Gaikwad child, wife to a Bhosale and I have been reduced to this... I will have to go with whoever comes along and stands in front of my basket. So tell me, what should I do?'

And with that, she went and sat down in her place.

The old lady said nothing. Customers who never came near her were now buying. To provoke Chandra, the men who bought from her were now at the old lady's basket. And the lady was quiet. The girl was moving her gorgeous body like lightning, turning and twisting it in ten different places as she spoke to the customers. And so evening came, and without saying a word, the old woman left.

The next day, she came alone. There was no basket on her head. There was no girl at her side. In order to taunt Chandra and get something started, one of the men said: 'No goods today? Or will they come later?' He did not mean bananas.

The old lady understood the hidden meaning of his words. She said, her voice filled with pain—'Son, she was a ghost. Yesterday, the one who was sitting next to me did not give my soul a moment's rest. I was frightened all the time. If my son Shiva finds out about this, he will not look upon me as his mother. And if the one for whom I did all this won't call me mother, what is the meaning of my life?

'Chandra is my daughter-in-law. She is the daughter of the ruling class and the daughter-in-law of royalty. Am I supposed to make a prostitute of her with my own hands? No, good sirs, that is never going to happen. I am going to the village…as long as my hands work, I will try to make my son's world a better one. And if I die…I will go quietly…'

And tears began to glisten in the old lady's eyes. Without wiping them away, she went to Chandra and putting a hand on her head, she said: 'Child, I made a mistake, Shiva's mother made a mistake. His wife is pregnant. I was greedy for a grandchild and in that greed, I made a mistake. I attacked a married woman. Forgive me. I could not see your young life, its suffocation, because of my anger. I could not see how you were burning through the day and the night…Sati Savitri brought her husband back from the doors of death. You should do the same. May God bless you…'

The old lady pressed her trembling lips together as she wept and quickly placed her hands on Chandra's head in blessing. And Chandra fell at the old lady's feet and kissed them repeatedly. With no control, her body was writhing and she was sobbing and saying, 'Aatya, please forgive this sinner. Please take me to your breast.'

'Let go, child, let go. Everyone makes mistakes. Get up, my girl. Get up.' And she hoisted Chandra up and sat her down. She wiped the young woman's face with her own pallu and said, 'Chandra, take care. Behave like a Bhosale daughter-in-law. I'm off.'

She did not look back as she walked away. Chandra watched her go with tear-filled eyes. And all day, the tears ran freely.

Revolt

TWO YEARS LATER, the reply came. Parbhu had asked that his son be given a job. And although he was now at death's door, here it was. His son, Jai, was studying for his matriculation. When he refused to take the job as a Bhangi, a wave of anger erupted against him. But he was adamant; even if the entire community rose up to oppose him, he would not take it. He was in full revolt against his parents who were insisting he give up his studies and become a Bhangi. He stood now, waiting for his father to say something so that he might attack him with the help of his powerful vocabulary. In the school and in the settlement, he had been able to defeat the great and the good in debate and even now, when his father was on his deathbed, he was intent on demolishing the old man's decision to make his son a Bhangi.

Lying wearily on his cot, Parbhu was trying to assess the mental state of his angry son who was standing by the foot of his cot. In his head, he was trying to find the words to dispel the white-collar dreams his son had been nurturing. His sixteen- or seventeen-year-old daughter-in-law, Shanti, was sitting on the bed, pressing his feet. She had drawn the edge of her pallu from across her head to her chest. And as always, she was beating her husband in the secret spaces of her head. She wanted to tell him to take her, to abandon his education, to get a job, to settle down and begin a physical relationship with her. Her mental pain communicated itself to her father-in-law almost as soon as she touched his feet. Taking courage from her touch, he began, 'Jai…'

Without giving his father an opportunity to say a word more, Jai shouted, his interior revolt now in full flight:

'Pitaji, whatever happens, I will not give up my education. I will not take up this job of a Bhangi that is being thrust upon me. In fact, when I finish my education and I am as wise as Socrates, I am going to destroy this inhuman practice of untouchability.'

This answer was a sharp sword slicing through all their hopes.

For here was a man who could snarl at his father like an animal when the latter lay on his deathbed; a man who could ignore the poverty and deprivation in his own home; a man, who though he was physically male, would not so much as look at his own wife. And for her part, his wife began to see him as stupid, unfeeling and intensely selfish. She began to look at him from behind the veil of her ghoonghat; and his physical beauty excited her. That she should be thinking such thoughts—and in the presence of her father-in-law—made her feel ashamed of herself. She bowed her head again and applied herself to pressing his feet.

This gentle service from his daughter-in-law stirred the old man's heart. He feared that after his death the girl might suffer even more; he feared that his son's complete refusal to look at his wife even by mistake would drive her to search for the comfort of another man's arms. These fears made him speak with no little bitterness and no less determination. 'Jai, can't you see the state we live in, the condition your mother is in? Don't you hear your wife's sighs?'

'Just for this I should become a Bhangi? Give up my education to clear up the dirt of the village? Carry filth on my head? If you wanted me to do that kind of work, why did you have me educated? Why did you let them light these lamps of independence, knowledge and humanity inside my mind?'

The yearning in his voice caused the old man's eyes to moisten in sympathy. He began to see his son's sorrow. But Shanti's mind filled with hatred for him. She saw her husband as a useless fellow. She cursed her own fate and began to weep, and Jaichand, full of the anger of rebellion, let out a roar of revolt.

'I am not going to do that job. I will never become a Bhangi.'

It was as if the revulsion he felt for the work he was being asked to do had turned into electricity and was coursing through this refusal. Shanti was reduced to ashes and the old man was scorched by the radiant heat of this sun. However, he persisted in trying to explain their situation.

'...But you are the son of a Bhangi. What problem can you have with doing this job? People pay to get these jobs, hundred, even a hundred-and-fifty rupees. And here you're getting one free. We need you to take this job. If you had a job, I might not be so near death. Your mother would not be reduced to a skeleton. This girl would not live in this state…'

'Where is it written that a Bhangi's son must become a Bhangi?'

'In our poverty. In our dharma. In our country.'

'What dharma? If it breaks a person and turns him into an animal, is that dharma? In this country that invests greater significance in a stone than in a human being? I will not heed such a dharma. If it has given us only this poverty, this deprivation, then it behoves us to reject it. But we are not going to do that. I will. Just let me pass my examinations…

'Until that time, let me go where I can beg for food… or sin for it…for the sake of my stomach.

'Those who do not have patience may feel free to commit such sins for their stomachs.'

Hearing this, the river of tears running inside Shanti's head turned to acid. Her hands stilled on her father-in-law's legs.

Fearing that the force of his hatred for the job might overheat his son's brain thus driving him to madness or to suicide, Parbhu tried for a more conciliatory tone to quell those terrifying visions.

'Do this job until you find another. You can go to night school. When you pass, and you find another job, you can give this one up.'

'I will not. If you want, I'll leave school. I'll rob or become a dacoit. But not this job…'

'It's not a Bhangi's job. The muqaddam has requested the boss. Your mother has fallen at everyone's feet. Go and see at least…'

'No one will listen. Even if one boss is Christian and the other one is Muslim, they will all only see me a Bhangi. They will never see me as an educated person. No one at school sees me as a student, Pitaji, only as a Bhangi. Nowhere in the world is there a country like this one, which persecutes you every step of the way. How much must we bear? How much must we swallow? Is this a country or a prison, a jail? And why must I, an innocent man, live the contempt-ridden, insult-filled life of a prisoner? Why endure this hell? Why? Why?'

Hearing his son's ear-splitting cry, the old man trembled. He looked at his son with compassionate eyes; seeing his father's tears and his shivering, Jaichand sat down. He began to stroke his father's chest with his clean, delicate fingers. He wiped his eyes. And feeling the love in those fingers, the old man drew his son's head down to his chest. He began to caress his son's head. Over the past few years, Jai, though he had lived in the same house, had grown aloof and had isolated himself; so now he simply let his head rest on his father's chest and allowed himself to enjoy the feeling of being loved. He felt himself to be a field now, a field that had been burning in the sun and was now drinking in the rain, releasing a fragrance and beginning to blossom. He felt himself opening up, and he began to tell his father of the uncountable dreams he had for his life.

'Pitaji, when I pass my exams, I am going to become a clerk. I'll go to college. I'll get my PhD. I'll make sure you all live happy, rich lives. And when the two of you go to your heavenly homes, the journalists will write stories about you. They'll say you were the parents of Dr Jaichand Rathod.'

The old man could not find the courage in his beleaguered heart to listen to his son's ramblings about his beautiful dream world of the future. He closed his tear-filled eyes and continued to stroke his son's head.

For years the love that had been suppressed under the boulders of their disagreements began to squeeze its way out. His son was no parasite. He loved his family but his heart was filled with zeal, with good intentions. That he should have wanted to deny such a jewel his education; that he should have shouted at him for refusing the job of a Bhangi caused him such terrible sorrow, that he began to murmur to himself:

'You should not have been born my son, not in this country. Your soul has suffered too much. I married you off young and tied you down. But now don't ruin this poor girl's life; she's as good as gold…Even if you're keeping her at a distance now because you want to finish your education, don't let it always be so… And don't behave badly with your mother…You never call her mother in public…You don't want to go anywhere with her. She longs to show off her well-built and well-educated son to all her worker-friends. But you avoid her as if she were a wild animal seeking your blood. How much she weeps about this. She keeps all her sorrows to herself. When she can't bear it any longer, she tells me or this poor child to ask you to change your ways…Jai, let her be a mother to you.'

Jai's eyes filled up at his father's words. He put a hand on his wife's shoulder and asked in a choked voice:

'Is this true, Shanté?'

Shanti ducked her head in embarrassment. This was

the first time he had spoken to her or touched her after he became a man. That made her very happy. The hatred she had begun to feel for him lessened. However, her mind had gone through a series of reversals. In a profoundly despairing voice, Jaichand began to say:

'What kind of culture is this? Where a man can treat the mother who gave him life with contempt simply because she does the work of a Bhangi? Where he can insult her and refuse to eat the food she cooks? If this culture had not created untouchability, I would not be the chief tormentor of my poor aged mother...'

He fell at her feet. She had turned to give him a piece of her mind but he was weeping and pressing her feet to his face. 'Forgive me, Ma, forgive me.'

This boy who would not eat what she had cooked even after she had washed her hands with soap was now kissing her dust-laden feet? What was this? Had he run mad? Her heart skipped a beat. She began to tremble. She wanted to speak to him but her tongue seemed to have cleaved to her palate.

'She'll fall over,' Shanti said, frightened and then startled by her own audacity, she ducked her head and sat down.

'Come, Aai,' he said and brought her outside.

'No, son, you don't have to go. Let's send Shanti. Let's ask about her,' said the old lady.

'Then who will cook for me? Who will serve me with her own hands?' and putting his hand on his mother's back, he urged her to walk with him. The happy awareness that her son did not hate her, that he loved her, was somewhat dispelled by his words, 'Who will cook for me? Who will serve me?' She dragged her feet a little as she walked.

But he was urging her forward. And watching his son make a bonfire of his dreams as he went forward with the resolution of a martyr, the old man began to burn with regret.

Bhani had collapsed completely. She was being dragged along like a log, impelled forward by her son's velocity.

This was how they came to be standing in the courtyard of the office. The Christian boss looked at Jai and Bhani.

Seeing the beautiful powerful youth who looked like something out of the Classical Roman era, he called to the muqaddam:

'Muqaddam!'

'Yes, sir?'

The muqaddam, who was assigning work, stopped to offer a namaste.

'Give him a cart.'

'A cart?'

'Yes, a cart. They asked for a mehtar's* job.'

'A cart?' Bhani was shocked.

---

*Mehtar is both a caste descriptor and an occupation. The two are used interchangeably since the traditional occupation of the mehtar caste was sanitation. According to *The Tribes and Castes of Central Provinces of India*, Vol I by R V Russell: 'The sweeper's calling is well-defined and under the generific term of Mehtar are included members of two or three distinct castes, as Dom, Bhangi and Chuhra; the word Mehtar means a prince or headman, and it is believed that its application to the sweeper by the other servants is ironical. It has now, however, been generally adopted as a caste name.' The Mehtars were listed as a Scheduled Caste under the Indian Constitution in 1950.

'A cart it is. When someone joins as a mehtar, they start with a cart,' said the boss, a cigarette clamped between his lips.

'He's studying for his Matric…'

'Let him. But he's a mehtar. And he's here to be a mehtar. Go.'

The boss had nothing more to say to Bhani. The educated children of Bhangis often came for jobs, impelled by their destitution. When they were faced with the terrible, demeaning work of the cart, they ran away, leaving the vacancy his to sell again. There were two vacancies like that. He would take a hundred rupees and give the job to someone for four months; and after that, he would get another hundred from someone else. This was the third such post from which the boss had earned a lot.

Jai walked quietly with the muqaddam. Behind them, carrying the burden of her pain, walked Bhani. Her fever had increased. Her face was pale. Her mouth was dry. She was sweating profusely. Her feet moved with effort and the belief that they were doing something criminal to her son was lacerating her heart, so full of maternal love.

The muqaddam and Jai arrived at an area in Ghatkopar. It was a crowded, tense area. There were a number of small and large buffalo stables there. These were surrounded by a throng of chawls and huts. This enormous population was served by thirty-two toilets. It was in front of this block of toilets that the muqaddam stopped and said:

'This is your job. Bring the cart here and go in and bring out the boxes and pour them into the cart. Then you have to clean the boxes. You will have to clean the toilets as well as the staircases and the area around. If you don't do the job well, out you go and the job goes back into the boss' pocket. Today it will seem horrible; tomorrow you'll be glad of the job. I'm off.'

And he walked off proudly.

Jai remained standing there. The little children had already fouled the place. Looking at those turds made gooseflesh break out all over his body and inside it, revolt brewed. He stood stock still, looking around him.

Looking at her son standing there like a statue, his proud eyes beginning to fill with tears, Bhani, tormented by shame, anger and self-hatred, said in a guilty tone:

'Son, you don't have to do this job. Go home. Go.'

'Why?'

'It's not work meant for you. It's for unlettered folk like us. It's for those who are already broken in mind, body, nose, forehead, broken everywhere, broken and dead.'

'So it's for you? That's…'

'Never mind, my son. Don't say it. Don't use these slippers to hurt your mother. Go. Go. We don't want such a job. We will not eat and drink and make merry over your body. I beg of you, go.'

He was looking at her. Controlling the wail that was rising inside her was making her lips and cheeks tremble. Tears were running from her eyes. Seeing this, he felt like crying too. But the fire of resolution running through him dried the tears. They simply would not get past his eyes. His revolutionary mind was now fighting the dharma and the nation. He had debated these issues with the nation and with the dharma. When the yellow flames merge with the red ones in a furnace, a series of muted explosions results; and this was what was happening inside him. Just then the shit cart arrived and stopped and the driver called out, 'Bhani, what are you doing here?'

She turned around to look. So that she would not come down the narrow passage between the blocks of sixteen back-to-back toilets, Jai went clattering down the stairs.

'Jai,' she called and her voice froze the blood of the listener, for it came from a shattered heart.

It was the sound of a mother forced to bear witness to the death of a child.

The stench emanating from the thirty-two toilets filled his throat. His breath was plucked from him. Darkness swam before his eyes. He closed them. Then he began to understand why his eyes had grown heavy, where his pain had come from. His brain was thrashing about like a fish thrown on burning sand, his veins seemed ready to burst open and were beating against his forehead and the back of his head, and it seemed as if someone had shoved a churn into his stomach and was rolling it about again and again and the nerves of his stomach seemed ready to rip their way out of his mouth. He closed his lips firmly. The strength went out of his legs, which had begun to tremble, so he stood still. He began to look around him with eyes peeled.

He turned his eyes to look at each tin under each toilet. Each glimpse brought fresh rigors to his body. His blood was boiling. There were thirty-two of them, each filled with filth, some surrounded by accumulated and rotting waste which was alive with maggots and flies; in one or two places there were blood-stained cloth, balls of used cotton wool, bandages and gauze strips...all this filled him with revulsion. His body trembled; his face was covered with sweat. He felt he was going to slip and fall. He felt he had to do something terrible, something destructive. He was Abhimanyu in the chakravyuha, surrounded by armed enemies. Were these the common enemies of all mankind or was it only the crime of having been born in this country, that meant one had to be thrust into this hell? And what kind of evil nation was this that any man should ask another to do such hateful work for money? And what kind of people would accept that it was their lot in life to do such work? How could they be willing to do this to make ends meet? Mankind, who has named everything in the world, who has created the Gods and the dharma, who has conjured up creation out of nothingness. Mankind...greater than all the five elements and more powerful. Man does this work...Why? Why? What demon does he fear? What terrible draught must he drink?

As blood gushes from a wound, the thoughts rushed from his head while the carter, tired of waiting for the load of filth, shouted:

'Arre, have you fallen asleep in there? Sonny, I have the whole village to clean up. Get on with it...Hurry up...'

He turned to look at the man calling out to him from above. Seeing his paan-stained lips parted in a smile, a violent flame was lit in Jai's light eyes. And the man above stepped back involuntarily: 'Deewaana!' (Mad man!)

Knowing that her son was standing there thinking, Bhani was herself a stone doll, petrified by shame and pain.

She slowly raised her feet and limped up to her son and with more strength than she had in her body, she unloosed her tongue and shouted, 'Ja...a...i!'

And then she slipped and fell, turning as white as a corpse, and so that she might not rise and come down herself, he jumped to it, grabbing a full tin and pulling it, but just then he found his fingers covered in shit. And again the hair rose all over his body. And though his mind was filled with revulsion, he hurriedly hoisted the pot to his shoulder. This blind hurry meant the tin shook and spilled. The contents spilled over, glug, glug, on to him. And just as a man who finds that a snake has coiled itself around him and has bitten him lets loose a scream of agony, Jai screamed, 'Aai!'

Hearing his cry, the carter who had been helping Bani sit up, looked down to see Jai standing in the pit of hell, and in a voice full of disgust, said, 'Idiot.'

Jai, filled with the destructive desires of revolt, began to run up the stairs. His anger and disgust at all that had happened made him almost unaware of the filth that was all over him. When he got to the top, he dropped the tin and was about to pounce on the carter when he saw his mother, sweat-soaked, corpse-pale, and said, 'Grab that.'

'Go on, throw it in. Don't dirty her up as well,' said the carter, disgusted at the boy, even as he looked affectionately at his mother. This disgust, caused the revolt, the hatred, the horror that was running through Jai's nerves to rise up within him. And so he took the tin he had brought up with him and threw it wherever it went, and then he grabbed the carter with both hands.

'Animal, are you going to teach me? Are you trying to rub salt in my wounds? Do you want to mock me?' and so saying, Jai began to beat him, his hands flying and falling with the intensity and fury of a monsoon storm.

As the sea in a storm whips the fishing boats again and again until it destroys them, he lashed out at the carter. The latter was shouting in an attempt to save his life, 'Help, help!'

The bhaiyyas who were tending the buffaloes came out with sticks in their hands. The folks from the chawl gathered. But none of them tried to stop the dangerous fight that had broken out between two mehtars. Unwilling to be polluted by touching either one, the North Indians stood with their sticks, unmoving. And the rest did not intervene for fear that they would come in contact with the village's accumulated shit. They simply watched as the two were locked in a death struggle.

Bhani, wailing like a cat, was wandering around them, screaming and crying, begging people to stop them.

When the carter fell at last, lifeless, a corpse, the rage began to recede from Jai's body. He hugged his mother to his chest and shouted: 'Maa, break my fingers...cut off my hands...slash open my body, throw away my corpse.'

As a man who has soaked himself with petrol begins to scream, a cry that tears through the heart, so Jai screamed.

And Bhani could only wonder if her son had gone mad; this shock made her teeth chatter.

The people stood and watched. But no one could make sense of the flame of revolt that was burning inside Jai. There was no way for them to understand it. For their minds had been murdered long ago by Manu.*

---

*Several attempts have been made to ban dry toilets such as the one described here. However, the law cannot be enforced, say activists, since the government is one of the major offenders.

Pesuk[*]

'OH YES, THE heart of a woman is a complete marvel. It is unparalleled, unequalled. It makes life rich and beautiful, as the dawn adorns the day. Savitri, for instance, made huge sacrifices to give her useless husband a son. To ensure his happiness, she climbed on to the pyre and was reduced to ash. And yet that evil creature could not see her greatness. The evil, hypocritical zamindar, Jaidev...' Kaka had wandered off to another topic. His powerful words had us enthralled but also confused. Sindhu's curiosity was further excited by his silence and she asked, 'What exactly did Jaidev the zamindar do, Kaka?'

'...I'm telling you. I was underground in those days. The British kept their eyes peeled but they couldn't catch me. They even offered a reward for my capture. The police tried to make my life hell but I would not be caught. And I kept doing my work. One day, in the darkest watch of the night, I had set out on one of my jobs. One of my friends was of the opinion that I should not take the predetermined route. For in that area there was a pesuk. It could peel a man like an orange and finish him off.

---

*A pesuk is an evil spirit generally in the form of a woman.

'That entire area was riven by fear of the pesuk. No man went out alone or even in pairs. The pesuk would not kill women; it would not even harm a hair on a woman's head. But if a man dared to go out, he would lose his nose, or so the legend went in that area. The fear of the pesuk had the jagirdar in such terror that he set ten men to guard his home, just to keep his nose intact. Only the women did not fear the pesuk; in fact the pesuk helped them; and it was this terrifying road that I had chosen. This was because I feared the police.

'That night of bewitching enchantment reduced all of creation to nothing; a strange secretiveness veiled all of nature. The high hills that could break the necks of the clouds and bring them down to earth, that could bear the sun's weight upon their shoulders, that were the first to salute the dawn, the hills that helped the revolutionaries and acted as their arms dumps, those very hills had been swallowed up by the darkness. This seemed to have descended from the heavens, seated on a chariot in the form of the God of Death. Those high hills and their deep shade admitted no details; the riverside area seemed black as tar and deeply fearful. Through that deep darkness, I walked with the only light coming from inside me. I quickened my pace. I had a loaded pistol in my hand and...

'Around a bend in the way, some rays of light showed up. I slipped behind a tree. The light was coming my way. This was no miracle of the new moon; it was not the Palanquin of the Vetaal*; it was a funeral procession.

---

*Around March-April, a stone image of the Vetaal, a deity associated with cremation grounds and death, is put in a palkhi

Only, many of the people who were accompanying the body on its final journey were armed. There was no music, no one was chanting or singing abhangas. The men were bearing arms. I had never seen armed mourners before, so I began to have some doubts. I got my pistol ready. Since there was no safe way out, it was best to stay where I was. But—

'The procession did not come forward. The mourners stopped where they burn the bodies. In a few seconds they had placed the body on the pyre. Wood was piled on top of the body and then the usual commotion about setting the pyre alight; now my doubts took on another shape. No Hindu cremation ever takes place so quickly, that much I knew. Now I thought I should approach.

'Since the men trying to light the fire were in a terrible hurry, the wood would not burn. Finally it did catch fire. And then in the darkness, a heart-rending wail arose. The men who had been scuttling about to light the pyre were startled by this. When the next wail arose, they simply began to run. Some dropped their lights and their weapons; some even fainted. Men were falling over themselves, slipping and running without once looking back. Watching this mad dashing about, a host of questions, rather like the ghosts and demons that are supposed to dance madly in front of the Palanquin of the Vetaal, began to swarm into my mind: weapons for a funeral procession? No musicians? Whose body? Why

---

and taken out in procession by the Wadars and the Mahars. The best-known literary Vetaal stars in the *Betalpachisi* that dates back to the eleventh century.

did that wail frighten the men so much? And who had let loose that shrill wail?

'It was the pesuk who had wailed! Once that idea raised its head inside me, it would not leave. Like a stick stuck in sticky mud, each step drove it deeper. I crept forward. The pyre was burning dimly in that frightening atmosphere. My eyes were fixed upon it. My ears were pricked up; but no human sound came from anywhere.

'From time to time, a log would burst and break. My pistol stayed drawn. I began to hurry as I walked up to the pyre. Then my hackles rose as if a snake had slithered over my body. My blood began to run with fire. My mind was filled with a weird feeling, sister to fear. I stopped and kept my eyes fixed on the pyre. For in front of it…

'…the pesuk was standing, or so my mind was screaming at me. My eyes were also ready to believe it, for the figure I could make out did not seem to have so much as a stitch of clothing on. All the men had fled by this time. I was standing still but my curiosity would not let me stay. To my surprise, my feet would not lift themselves up—and my mind was shouting: *Pesuk, pesuk…*

'Assuming that this was a pesuk, I moved forward. To keep my nose safe, I had my pistol at the ready. As I neared the pyre, the apparition's heart-breaking cry rose again, making my hair stand on end. The scream had such an odd force to it, that I began to feel some sympathy for the pesuk. But my steps did not quicken. And…

'Another miracle happened. The pesuk, who had been standing at the head of the pyre, suddenly vanished. I began to rub my eyes as I walked; but I could see nothing but the pyre. As cold pierces one, as a knife driven to the heart, this lament was terrifying. I had never heard anything like it. Inside me, fire broke out. Today I am seventy-five, but those flames have not been put out. My anger has not been extinguished. Nor do I lay down my arms…'

And then suddenly Kaka stopped speaking. This made us uncomfortable. Like all the rest sitting in the room, my gaze too was held by his magnificent face. Looking at him, I began to think of the auspicious elephant of Lord Buddha. Staring at Kaka's face, Sindhu was alarmed by the sound of the clock striking. Like me, no one could say a word. Everyone was looking at Kaka's bulky frame. We were all completely sold on his mysterious story.

Like the thunder that heralds the monsoon, Kaka's voice resounded in the room…

'My eyes were fixed on the pyre. I could not look away even though I tried. Suddenly the pesuk, who had vanished, appeared again and began to walk around the pyre. Sometimes it would fold its hands and touch its forehead. It was mumbling and murmuring in sorrow, sometimes muttering in rage. Seeing how much it seemed to love the dead person reassured me. The attraction we all have to the horrible, to that which is marvellous or supernatural, was drawing me to the pyre. My state was like that of a moth drawn to a flame. And to meet the pesuk, I quickened my steps.

'Stopping its circumambulation of the pyre, the pesuk did a full prostration in front of it, and while it was dragging a flaming log from the fire, I stopped in front of it.

'And at that second, the wail began again and angrily

the pesuk came for my nose, dropping the wood, in order to rip out my throat, to tear me limb from limb and to throw them asunder; it leapt at me, its claws bared, a bolt of lightning. I shrank into myself and the pesuk missed, its leap carrying it falling and tumbling past me until it landed in a heap. I leapt away and with the same speed turned to attack it.

'But a single look into the pesuk's eyes drained the strength from my muscles. My terrified mind began to protest. My careful attention was destroyed. My body shrank into itself as a furnace of old memories began to burn.

'For this was no pesuk. It was a woman of the kind that created great heroines such as Sita and Savitri; she had the strength and power of Mother Ganga…the kind of truth and beauty that is as immortal as the sun; it was that evil Jaidev whose disgusting brain and whose cruelties had made her as terrible as a ghost.'

Despite his best efforts, Kaka's tears began to flow and his words remained in his mouth. Since he was one of India's most daring revolutionaries and had spent considerable time underground during the British Raj, I was shocked to see this sensitive side of him.

'Her dark hair had turned the colour of mud. Its beautiful velvety texture had gone; it was now matted and tangled. Where on her rosy forehead there had once been kumkum, there were dark bruises. Her head had been branded, and the scar ran from her eyebrows to the top of her head. Her straight nose was broken; her upper lip writhed with anger, like a severed snake's tail. Rage contorted her face and made her ugly; it made my heart burn even as my mind was struggling desperately with what I had seen. Both her breasts had been cut off. The left one, either by an oversight or because the milk had been flowing when it was cut off, had some small lumps of flesh still dangling, and as they had dried there, they looked like worms clinging to her body. Her entire body had been devastated.

'She was Jaidev's sixth wife!

'Seeing how her beautiful body had been savaged, I wanted to murder Jaidev; I wanted his ugly and evil soul to be ground into the mud to rot; I wanted to bandage her wounds with a handkerchief spun from the melting strands of my heart. I shouted at her, "Savitri, where is that devil?"

'Seeing my rage and the loaded pistol in my hand, her once-mild eyes became like fire. She turned her wrathful gaze upon me. I tossed the sheet I had been carrying for myself over her, for she was completely naked—this woman who had once been so humble and gentle and respectable.

'Now more terrible than a demon, Savitri was reduced to screaming and wandering around a corpse in the night… Was it the memory of being a beautiful woman once? Was that what had brought this on? Or was it my misguided attempt to restore some semblance of humanity to her?

'Now she was standing still in the dark. I began to approach her. I had much to say to her. I wanted to hear what she had to say. I wanted to give her whatever she wanted. But as soon as I got close, she shrieked and ran into the river. Her haste made the water splash and bubble. She was reduced to nothing as the life came out of her.

'She got to the other bank and the birds in the trees there began to flutter and flap and call restlessly. She was running as if out of all control. I was watching silently. I was going mad, thinking about her. I had decided to destroy Jaidev. For a long time, I stood there. Then my attention was drawn to one side. Next to me, another pyre had been built. I could see there was no corpse on it. A terrible fear seized me. For whom was this pyre? And whose body was burning on the other one? I went forward again.

'"Savitri, wait…" I opened my mouth to shout but the words would not emerge. For suddenly, I became aware of my underground status. The shout died and fell back into my heart. It is there, alive still…

'But even if I had called, she would not have come. She would not have spoken with me. She had no need of anyone, no need of anything. She was now devoid of humanity, she was like an animal with a bestial cruelty. Like animals, she had a distrust of humans. She feared women and attacked men. She was no longer human, so she did not need clothes. She had not taken the sheet I offered her and she did not speak to me. Had she still been human…had she been the old Savitri…but no… she was not human…no.'

Kaka swallowed a huge ball of sorrow. As if in a daze, he kept running his hand over his brownish hair. His state shocked us, and it seemed from Sindhu's quivering lips that another emotional jolt would make her ululate.

'She was no human, this mistake… She was a woman and as long as her child was alive, she had been in hiding in the hills. When Jaidev had killed him, she was set free. She became as destructive as a storm. She became as merciless as the monsoon.

'She began her attacks with her father-in-law. She set upon him and three of his men. One of them who was injured went home and died. His family buried him but the next day, they found the ground disturbed.

'The body had been dug up and its nose cut off. This was the first male nose to go. After this she began her attacks on men and their noses, and soon a legend took shape and a ghost began to haunt the men. In order to protect their noses, men stopped going out alone. Some roads were closed to travellers for days on end. This did not stop her. She went after them persistently, a ghost relentless in her pursuit.

'...And as for her husband, Jaidev, he was on her hit list too. He had assumed that she was dead and had married a seventh time; because for the three years that her child had been alive, no one had seen her. But when this child, born of her immeasurable sacrifice and of her terrible ordeal, had gone, she had begun her merciless and determined attacks.

'Like a shadow, she had stuck to Jaidev. When she felt like it, she would come and take hold of him. He was so terrorized that whatever he was doing—eating, taking medicines, whatever—he would protect his nose with his fist. He died a thousand deaths, a death every minute. And yet she pursued him, intent on his nose. Incessantly, she worked on destroying him economically. She wanted to leave his mansion a ruin, a burnt-out hollow.

'Many men had fallen ill as Jaidev had.

'And all this he had brought upon himself out of his

desire to be a father, to keep his lineage going. His first wife had committed suicide after only a few days and freed herself. The second had gone mad and had been made into a prisoner of the wada. His third wife—she ran away with another. The fourth went home to her parents and could not tell them anything, for she had lost her mind. The fifth was a mute. She could not say anything. Like the fourth, she too was unable to bear his cruelty. Which was why he felt his line was in danger. To hold his head up in society, he felt he needed a son. None of his wives could give him that. One killed herself, one went mad, some ran away and some died on the way and yet the rumours would not die but kept increasing every day. And so he married a beautiful woman in order to save his pride, his honour.'

'Who would give such a man their daughter's hand in marriage?' I asked angrily and Kaka went on: 'People do… Jaidev was the owner of hundreds of acres of land. There was never any shortage of food or money in his house and he was a high-class Kshatriya. The fathers of these girls were dazzled by the wealth and then there was their poverty and their pride in their caste. Savitri's father was no different. He wanted a rich boy. And Jaidev gave him wealth, so he dispatched his daughter to hell. For a son, another marriage.

'He knew and everyone knew that a delicate, flower-like girl such as Savitri would not live there. She would die…but she did not die. For months on end, she survived. And her father began to grieve. When she delivered a child, it was worse than death. For she had blackened the name of his family.

'...Had she killed herself, they could have used the money to build her a fine memorial. Her life as an ideal wife could have become the stuff of legend. But Savitri had sinned in order to become a mother.

'Jaidev had wept. He had clutched her feet; and finally he had threatened to kill himself. An Indian wife will bear everything but she will not bear widowhood. Being a widow is a terrible punishment...far worse than corporal punishment...Savitri agreed. She agreed to become a mother.

'That was a farce. When his masculinity had been proved, he no longer had any use for her or the child. He began to insult her. The result of this was that the secrets of the house came spilling out into the open. They spread as if on the wings of the wind. And so Jaidev's newly restored respectability began to develop flaws. Jaidev went mad and Savitri found no refuge from him. But she continued to endure and finally...

'She, her son and her son's father were caught as they tried to escape. Savitri was made to pay for her sins. Nothing happened to the boy and the boy's father. For he was one of Jaidev's relatives. Then as much disgrace as could be was piled upon Savitri. Because Jaidev was alive, her head was not shaved. But she was shorn and the strands that remained were drenched in sindhur to discolour them. Then she was taken out in procession. All those who danced and rejoiced in this procession were to lose their noses later...

'Because of this procession, Jaidev was accepted as warrior, his masculinity affirmed. All doubt was laid to rest, his Kshatriya status confirmed. His honour grew.

Like a Chakravarti, a king of kings, his fame spread in all directions and so he was able, once again, to get himself a bride who was even more beautiful.'

Kaka's words began to trail off. Our hearts were burning with rage. Sindhu's anger sparked in her eyes. And when she spoke, it was as if she were shouting:

'Whose funeral pyre was it, Kaka?'

'I'm telling you that, child,' he said with a boundless love and then in a harsh voice, he said: 'Child, like you, that was the question I asked too. Two pyres? For whom? But when I got to the village I found out it was for Jaidev!'

'Jaidev?' we shouted as if in one voice.

'Had Savitri got his nose too?' Sindhu asked in an extreme anger.

'In order to prevent her from cutting his nose, the pall-bearers were armed and the musicians had been dispensed with. But even so, like a demon, she appeared and the men ran away, and the enmity ended,' Kaka stopped, but we were not at peace.

'Did she cut his nose off or no?' Sindhu demanded

'She commited Sati. She had not cut off his nose.'

'She didn't?' My heart sank irreversibly.

'Yes. How great is the Indian woman! What a treasure trove of humanity she is! Even death must bow to her.'

Kaka wiped his eyes. His hands were trembling and our hearts were beating fast.

When I Hid My Caste

WHEN THE DIFFICULTIES visited upon me after I concealed my caste come to mind, memory ignites a furnace in my heart. My head begins to ache as if it is about to burst; in this luck-forsaken country, human beings should not be born as Dalits. If and when they are, they must bear such sorrow and such disrespect as would make death seem an easier option, making a cup of poison a Dalit's best friend. For even nectar rots in one's heart and what is left is a rage, sharper and more cruel than a sword. This is the extent of the mental and emotional atrocities that I had to bear. If I had continued to live there, continued to hide my caste, the anxiety would have driven me mad. And so it was a good thing that I came to Mumbai, for on the night of pay day, at Ramcharan Tiwari's home, I was robbed. And one of the thieves had announced that I had been hiding my caste. And Ramcharan Tiwari beat me to his heart's content. And Kashinath Sakpal saved me from that immense rage.

This is how it came about.

At first light, I got down at Udhna Station* and was

---

*Udhna is now a suburban area of Surat, Gujarat. At the time of writing, it was probably a village.

walking to the engine shed. The joy of having got a job had made my mind as frisky as spring, as brave as rain. This sense of well-being had left me with no fear of anyone. No man was a stranger. I had not a care in the world. I was sure that every word I spoke would bring victory, every step I took would bring springs of fresh water spurting from the ground. For I had spent the night in the train, dreaming up a wonderworld of happiness.

So there I was, flowing like a morning breeze, when I saw a group of workers in front of me and called out to them, bringing them to an abrupt halt. From among them, Boiler-Fitter Ranchhod asked in Gujarati, 'What's up, brother?'

In chaste and elegant Gujarati, I introduced myself. Ranchhod was immediately ready to rent me a room and the workers with him began to look at me with admiration. They were taking in, with a look of awe, my coat, topi, dhotar, Kolhapuri slippers, the book of Mayakovsky's poems in one hand and the trunk to which my bedding was tied. The respect on all their faces, their curiosity, all this added to the joy I felt in getting a job. My mind, filled with this happiness, was like a woman dreaming of her lover. I could have got lost in all this happiness but then in a hesitant voice, Ranchhod asked, '...But what is your caste?'

I roared like a thunderclap on hearing this: 'Why do you ask me my caste? Can you not see who I am? Me, I am a Mumbaikar. I fight the good fight, I give my life in the defence of the right. I have freed India from bondage and I am now her strength. Got that? Or should I go over it again? Do you want it in verse?' Still buoyed up by my joy, I growled and walked on. For my mind, dreamstruck, was already racing ahead of me.

Behind me I could hear the pair of them muttering to each other.

'Arre Ranchhod,' said Devji, 'don't let this one get away. Don't lose the rent. He's a Marathi maanus. And a fearless one too. Possibly a Brahmin, maybe Kshatriya. Call him back. Go. Run after him.'

But bruised by my attack, Ranchhod would not come near me. He asked Devji to approach me on his behalf. Listening to this frightened chittering, I felt that all these people seemed small enough to fit into my pocket.

Finally, Ranchhod made a tentative approach. 'Now look here, don't get angry. When we meet a stranger, we always ask him his caste. This is the way in our country. I've as good as rented you the room. Will five rupees a month be okay?'

Devji interrupted: 'Brother, one can eat mud with a caste brother, but one shouldn't attend a feast with someone of a lower caste. A man like you is not going to live with some poverty-stricken dhedas, is he? Nor are you going to lose what you've earned by living with thieves.'

'You shouldn't speak that way in front of me, a new citizen of a new Bharat. We're all the creators of the new nation. There are no dhedas, no poor, no Brahmins.'

'My mistake.'

'Indeed a mistake, a mistake indeed. Words like that made a rich country like ours into a beggar. Got it?'

'Yes, but what about the room? Will you take it?'

Ranchhod was almost begging in his desperation.

'I'll think about it and let you know.'

'Think? Think about what? It's a lovely room. There's a well near it, full of sweet water. And mango trees around it. Every day, you'll see birds, birds of many colours. And you'll have birdsong. Do we have a deal?' His helplessness and this desperate sales pitch pleased me so much that I agreed. Delighted, he issued an immediate invitation. 'Let's have some tea.'

'Go on ahead. I'll follow,' I said. He obeyed, taking all the people he had with him. When we had crossed a line of railway bogeys, ducking under some, skipping past others that were being shunted away, we came to a grease-laden, soot-stained wagon in which they had a canteen that served tea and snacks.

There wasn't much room to sit inside. Even so, he rushed in and waved to me to enter and just as he was doing this, what should I hear but a voice like the cruel crack of a pistol-shot: 'Mahar.'

'M'har?' Ranchhod asked, turning his head and shrinking into himself. And my mind, which had been soaring like the Garuda*, was brought crashing to the ground. The joy, washing over my body, dried up. The tingly bubbles in my bloodstream evaporated. The words of our earlier conversation danced like demons in front of my eyes. I stood there, rooted to the spot, like a stone rammed into the earth.

Someone in the canteen had found me out; he had picked me out as one might pick out a stone from raw rice. Even as I was trying to decide how to surmount this question, Ranchhod's question fell upon my ears:

---

*Garuda means eagle but it is also the mount of Lord Vishnu. Perhaps both meanings were intended. Perhaps not. I leave it to the reader to decide.

'Tiwari, what does "Mahar" mean?'

And Tiwari replied from his half-knowledge: 'Mahar means Maharashtrian. They are like Shivaji the Great; warriors.'

'No Panditji, not like that. I'm one of Dr Ambedkar's party, of his caste. My name is Kashinath Sakpal, of Mumbai, Kala Chowky.'

Kashinath's rising voice inspired me, heartened me. The panic that invaded my heart quietened.

But Tiwari got it. Oh, he got it.

'Means an Untouchable.'

'You're right on target, Pandit Bhaiyyaji,' said Kashinath with a snigger.

And Tiwari roared in a rage: 'Smash the dirty dheda.'

'Get him,' they screamed, all those sitting in the canteen.

Kashinath set down the cup that had just touched his lips; he stuck both his hands in his pockets, cocked his head, inflated his chest and roared at them, a powerful, sensational roar: 'Come on then. Let's have you. Tiwari, come on. Hey, Ranchhod. Oy oldies, you come on too. Hey fatso, that means you too. Come on, all of you, any of you, however many of you. One? Two? Three? Come on then.'

No one got up. They sat there, frozen, fearful, staring at Kashinath. Kashinath began to feel the courage he was showing. He warned them, arrogantly: 'I'm off then. I'll tell your foreman a thing or two about the Constitution of India. And that will land you all in jail. I'll get you thrown out of your jobs. Out you'll go, like ants flicked away.'

He strode out, his steps like thunder, still spewing, still railing, ranting, talking big.

Inside, all the men were terrified into silence. Of them all, Nanaji Panchal, a hirsute black man looked the most uncomfortable. He was looking straight at the foreman's office. And then he broke the spell. Jumping to his feet, he shouted. 'Run. That Untouchable from Mumbai can't get to the foreman or we'll all lose our jobs. We'll be screwed. Run.' Grumbling and grunting, they bumbled out. Seeing how scared they were, Tiwari shouted: 'Sit down. I am here. I'll talk to my brother and straighten him out. Sit down...'

Since his brother was the foreman clerk, this reassured some of them. They even began to speak again. Then every man Jack of them was spewing filthy abuse and began to walk towards the engine shed. They were conspiring to get rid of Kashinath and I was so disheartened, so saddened, so reduced by their rage that I decided to return to Mumbai without further ado. I felt disgusted and disturbed but then I remembered how poor we were, and like a sick ox, I lowered my head and made for the foreman's office.

Seeing my bowed head and disordered gait, Devji approached me, concerned. 'Thakur, are you all right? You running a fever? Give me your bag. Go on then. You have to become that Untouchable's senior. He's as terrifying as a ghost. I'll look after your bag. There are lots of thieves around these parts and they are mostly these Untouchables.'

'No need.' I was terrified because I had hidden my caste and I could see his caste prejudices clearly, so I refused his support and encouragement. I was now the condemned man walking to the gallows. I made it to the steps of the foreman's office somehow and stood a while, lost in thought, all awareness of the body abandoned.

And then running down the stairs, victory in his bouncing bound, came Kashinath. His speed shocked me. I grabbed his arm and said, 'Wait. Tell me.'

But Kashinath was a whirlwind now; he freed himself with a jerk and pulling the knife out of his pocket, he said: 'Get away from me. I'll finish you off.'

'Aaho, I only wanted to hear what you went through. I'm also from Mumbai, like you…' Ranchhod was now within earshot, so I did not complete the sentence as I had meant to: '…and of your caste as well'. He told me, shouting, cursing, abusing and then he was off again, at the pace of a dust-devil.

I was so enraged at hearing about the indignities heaped upon him that I climbed the stairs, determined to quit my job in protest. Like a condemned man with the noose around his neck, I went and stood near the desk of Mataprasad Tiwari, foreman-clerk. Next to Mataprasad Tiwari, perched on a stool, was Ramcharan Tiwari. Both brothers' faces were red with rage. There was violence in their eyes. I looked at them and prepared for war, prepared to die.

'Hey, what were you saying to that unruly Untouchable?'

To shatter this arrogance to pieces, I said: 'Who is Untouchable? Fire is untouchable. The sun is untouchable. Death is untouchable. The five basic elements in their ideal forms are untouchable.'

'What do you mean? All this Mumbai talk…'

Since I had no care to keep my job, my words had the sharpness of a sword. 'I am from Mumbai. I am a graduate of the University of the Revolution. The people whom Manu rejected, whom he would have consigned to the dust-heap, who brought this great country its freedom, were those from my city. I am one of those great worker-warriors. My hands are the wheels of Bharat's progress,' I said in chaste, Sanskritized Hindi.

'What?' he asked, gobsmacked. Ramcharan's eyes filled with surprise. I repeated my answer.

'Don't listen to that Untouchable and serve me that city shit,' he said. 'I'm Mataprasad.'

I had decided to shed his blood and let the job go. So I said: 'I am the artisan of the new joys of the common man. I am a warrior in the cause of humanity. I am willing to give my life for it. I have a name. I have a city: Mumbai.'

'Don't talk shit,' he hollered.

'Not talking shit,' I said. 'I merely recite the new mantra of the new nation. With a new language, I inscribe a new nation.'

'Shut up. Talk sense or…'

'This is sense. I am a citizen-worker. I am among those who will lead Manu's backward nation to glory. I am a poet.'

'You? A poet?' Ramcharan's face was flooded with delight. He was gazing at me with a new admiration. I could not disappoint him, no way could I disappoint him. I said gently: 'Yes, Tiwariji.'

'Wah, wah,' Ramcharan hopped off his stool and

advanced upon me, both hands extended to take mine, when the irascible Mataprasad barked: 'Ramcharan!'

Thwarted, Ramcharan sat down again and Mataprasad asked, disdain dripping from his voice: 'Your name?'

He dipped his pen into the inkpot and suddenly I felt greedy for my job. And once again, thinking of my poverty-stricken home, I began to regret my earlier intemperate behaviour. To hold on to my job, I told him my name as politely and respectfully as possible.

When he wrote down my name I felt even sorrier for the way I had spoken to him. I felt so bad, I said: 'Forgive me.'

He was pleased by this and taking the high road, he pretended to be as big as possible and said: 'You speak Hindi almost as well as we do, like a Brahmin.'

Trying to match this display of generosity, I said as respectfully as possible: 'Sir, Hindi is the language of Tulsidas, of Kabir, of Niralaji and Premchand.'

This answer pleased the simple, sympathetic Ramcharan and he smiled. Mataprasad growled, 'Where are your certificates?'

I stood there, thinking for a moment and then affecting an air of unconcern, I said sweetly: 'I forgot them at home.' I wanted to see if I could get away with this.

'How much have you studied?'

'Non-Matric. I liked art and literature too much to want to study further.'

'That's why our people remain backward. That's why these low castes, these Chamaars and the like, get ahead. They become officers, even ministers. They have so many facilities in the Railways that tomorrow if that low-caste

Kashinath wants he can become a clerk. He too is a non-Matric. You will both begin as cleaners but one day he will rise to foreman or driver or controller. So get those certificates sent to you, understand?'

'Yes sir,' I said, oozing false humility. I salaamed him and decided that if no one mentioned the certificates again, I wasn't going to bother showing them.

'Go. You came after him but I've still made you the senior. Ranchhod told me about you. And look, don't hang around with Ramcharan too much. Poetry has ruined him. Off with you now.'

I came down and was about to pick up my trunk when Ramcharan popped up to take it from my hand.

'Hand it over. You're my guru from this day forth. You must explain poetry to me.'

This display of devotion frightened me a little. But he continued talking to me with great happiness, as if he had encountered Lord Rama. My own spirit, so accustomed to insult, so sickened by it, began to blossom. I was forgetting my error, and just as I began to talk to him on these easy terms, the rage-rich voice of Kashinath fell upon my defenceless ears and began to drag me back until I stopped: 'I am a Mahar but that does not mean I'm going to clean human shit and piss from the walls.'

'That's just what you will have to do. You will clean it up,' said the low-caste muqaddam, merely following Mataprasad's orders. Ramcharan saw this and was happy. And I could no longer conceal my uncase.

Kashinath was facing down the muqaddam and shouting in his face. Many workers had gathered to watch the fight. They were encouraging the muqaddam to stand his ground. And in order to prevent Kashinath from losing his job on the very first day, I went up to the muqaddam and said, 'These menial jobs should not be given to educated workers. You should assign these tasks to those who have no skills.'

Tiwari interrupted angrily, 'Which means that poor, old, uneducated Brahmins should do them? A veritable sage!' Many of the spectators were happy at this answer and turned on me. Some looked at me with suspicious eyes. Those words, 'a veritable sage', had hurt. But I made no reply. I was afraid of those suspicious eyes. But since I had to say something in return, I said: 'Tiwari, the youth of this country have always been its priceless and immortal wealth. With the five elements, they represent the sixth force. Our unfortunate and poor country is the only one that treats them with such disrespect. Which is why you see nothing but sorrow in all ten directions.'

No one liked what I said; contrariwise, many seemed to be bubbling over with the desire to ask what my caste was. Seeing this, a bomb exploded in my stomach. My heart was breaking, thinking about Kashinath. But he was still fighting with great determination. The muqaddam was not at liberty to listen; and all the workers had turned against Kashi. There was an urs* of pain in my heart as I came forward to say something.

And after this first day, every day that dawned was a mountain of grief that I was forced to carry on my head,

---

*An urs is held to commemorate the death of a Sufi saint, generally at his last resting place or dargah. This is as much a time of mourning and memorializing as it is a time of celebration for the gift of the saint and the gift of music. This is such a beautiful image, I had to retain it.

even as its weight crushed me to powder. Kashinath too was always being skewered. He picked a fight every day. That meant many of the workers treated him with enmity. Even his smallest mistakes were not tolerated. And his response to this ill-treatment was to look upon everyone with suspicion. Almost helplessly, like a madman, he would make war upon the wind. He began to carry a knife in his pocket. I could understand this helplessness and this rage and it burned my heart. I did not want this son of poor parents to come to grief in a strange land and so I would try to save him. I would try to keep the peace. I would meet him on the quiet and try to explain things to him. I was taking this much trouble because I did not want him to get so angry that he might stab someone and kill him. And I had to be very careful not to let other people see my sympathy for him. This cautiousness made me curse myself as a weak and timorous idiot.

And simultaneously, I began to treat everyone with the utmost care. Where I had once spoken with the freedom of the blowing wind, now I measured every word and considered its effects. Like a frightened rabbit, I tried to keep people at bay. I, who had once bathed in the crowded river of Mumbai's humanity, who had watched people as silently as a butterfly so that I might know them better, was now forced to crouch, weeping, in the cruel dark in order to conceal the secret of my caste. I would be forced to hold Ramcharan, who held me in high esteem, at arm's length.

And though my behaviour hurt him, he still did not abandon me. Every day, he would come up to me at least ten times. Every Sunday, he would invite me to eat a meal with him, his invitation whole-hearted, his insistence increasing to the point where he was almost in tears. And I turned him down each time with the same adamantine refusals that would set him off and he would curse and swear at his brother. His devotion and love would set off explosions in the quiet of my own home.

And so, holding my tongue and bearing the blows, I got through the days until it was pay day. I wanted now nothing more than to quit and so I put in a request for leave. Since I said I wanted to go and collect my certificates, Mataprasad immediately approved it. Somehow Ramcharan got to hear of this. And like a poor beggar, he began to follow me about with one prayer on his lips: Please come and eat at my home on pay day. And finally worn down by his extreme insistence, I agreed.

We got our pay. The question of whether to keep the job or give it up, a question that I had thought was dead, reared its head again. The poverty of my home might have resuscitated it. I began to feel the need for a job. And so I grew uncomfortable. I lost myself in the attempt to make a decision by sitting in the dark of my room and thinking. I smoked cigarette after cigarette. But I could not bring myself to accept the disrespect that would follow any revelation of my caste. And even as I was plagued by these anxieties, Kashinath's voice came to my ear: 'Masthur…'

'Yes Kashinath, come in.' The man who was willing to raise hell in the traditional wilderness of caste inequality could not bring himself to enter his caste-fellow's home. He stood outside.

'Come, come, I'm also a…' The proud young man's

shame at coming into the room of a caste-brother left me disconcerted. The truth came to the tip of my tongue but remembering the threat Ranchhod had made, I kept silent. And the tears that would not flow backwards had to be stanched with the edge of my dhoti.

'Masthur, if you had not been there to save me from all these fights, to protect me even, I would have killed both those demons—that Ranchhod and the poet Ramcharan. And then what would have happened to my aged parents and my wife?

'Masthur, I am terribly hot-tempered by nature. My elder brother-in-law was evil. He would torment my sister every day. He would beat her. Watching her being beaten and harassed every day, I would be filled with such rage, I would not be able to taste my food. When I was in my Matric year, the torture increased. To get him sorted out, I joined a gang of hoodlums. I grew close to them and I got him beaten up. He escaped death, for I meant him to die at my hands. And from that time, I dropped out of school.

'Masthur, I'm going to quit this job. I'm going to Mumbai. I'll take what work I can get. I'll finish my SSC. I'll go to college. I'll become a lawyer. No, now, I do not plan to die a worker. This life, this terrible life…'

As he said these words, shining tears fell from his eyes. As Kashinath of the sword-sharp mind bared his soul and its strife to me, I felt my heart fill too.

'Sakpal, I am going to quit too. Staying here means a living death, a life screwed over by death. Let's leave together. I also want to share my sorrows with you. Kashi, I am also a…' I was about to ask his pardon and tell him the story of how I had hidden my caste, when seeing Kashinath standing in the door near me, Ranchhod, already enraged at the disrespect shown to him, said with an animal's unthinking fearlessness, 'What's going on here? Since you're thinking of going to Mumbai tomorrow, are you going to pollute my room with your presence today?'

'Idiot, he's pulling your leg,' I said but Kashinath, driven mad by the constant attacks, went for Ranchhod. Ranchhod returned hurriedly to his room. Seeing the effect that the demon of casteism had had on Kashinath, the bottom dropped out of my heart. I rushed after him and caught hold of him and the aggression drained from his body. He dropped his entire weight on my shoulder and began to weep as a child might. And after a while, he took out a knife and vanished into the darkness.

Frightened by this, I peered into the darkness, knowing that I should locate and stop him. But I was rooted to the spot. I did not have the desire to turn on the lights nor to go and have dinner. This terrible glimpse of casteism had torn my heart to pieces.

'Ustad…' It was Ramcharan, bounding up as playful and happy as a summer breeze. Hearing his voice, Ranchhod came out with more choice abuses for the 'dhedas'; and when Ramcharan asked him what the matter was, he told him, with suitably violent gestures, what had happened and tried to lambaste me. He began to cast doubt on my caste as well. This made Ramcharan angry with him. Ranchhod began to accuse Ramcharan of false and baseless pride in his Brahmin birth. Ramcharan returned the compliment, accusing Ranchhod of boasting about the special qualities of Kshatriyas. And while they were fighting this battle, I went into the room and packed my trunk and my bedding and came out. I stood in front of Ranchhod's door and gave his wife the rent and started walking away.

At which point, Ramcharan abandoned the argument and came up behind me and said somewhat angrily, 'I have invited you to eat with me. I was going to come and fetch you. You said you would come. And yet, you're leaving without saying a word to me?'

I looked in his direction without a word. And then lowered my head and walked into the darkness.

'Ustad, tell me what happened. Did Ranchhod show you disrespect? Did he hit you? Tell me. Just tell me. I'll break his legs.'

I shook my head to indicate that nothing had happened and his throat seized up. Standing where he was, he raised both his arms to the sky in irritation and in a voice that was overwhelmed with emotion, he said: 'How many times did I beg you not to associate with that Untouchable?'

'Why? Both of us are sons of the same soil, sons of the same language. The sky above him, the earth beneath him, they're the same as what's above and beneath me.'

'You soar like an eagle. Come down to earth. We're ordinary labourers here.'

'Which is why we are the artisans of the new, which is why we have a responsibility to life!'

'Ustad, come home with me.'

'Ramcharan, forgive me. I have swallowed far too much poison today. I cannot absorb it into my system. So not now. Do me a favour and walk with me. I have something important to tell you.' I was about to tell him about hiding my caste.

'No, no, Guruji. Saraswati will be very offended. She has been cooking all day…'

'No.' Even as I said this, he turned and prepared to touch my feet. Seeing the depths of his devotion, I was humbled and said, 'Let's go, buddy. For your love, I am prepared to face death. Let's go.'

As we stood quietly in front of his room, he cried out in great happiness: 'Saraswati, come out and welcome our guest.'

Saraswati, who had been waiting for us, came out, her anklets tinkling. Over my protests, this fair, slender, black-haired woman, bright-red sindhoor in her hair, clutched the end of her sari-pallu in her hands and touched the feet of a man who was lower than her husband, younger than he, of a less socially acceptable complexion. Then she left. And seeing the devotion of an Indian wife for her husband started a storm in my head.

Immediately afterwards, she came out with a bucket of hot water, a small bowl of oil and a lump of soap, and with great enthusiasm Ramcharan said to me—'Sit there. Have a bath, I'll rub you down with oil.'

Somewhat shy, I said, 'Bhabhi made a mistake when she touched my feet. Now I won't tolerate any of this.'

'What of that?' Saraswati asked from behind the door. 'Our guest is as our God.'

'No, no, I'm half-dead already. Any more and I'll be dead soon.'

She laughed. I washed my arms and legs and went in. Then it occurred to me that Ranchhod might have

added his own two bits to the story of my encounter
with Kashinath and that this might be the reason why
Ramcharan wanted me to have a bath. As soon as that
occurred to me, I said, 'Shall we eat outside?'

'No, you are the guru of a Brahmin,' he said, taking
my hand and drawing me into the house. 'Come inside.'

'But I am not a Brahmin…'

'Never mind, you are my guru.' He sat me down on a
low stool. Saraswati sat in front of us, fanning us in such
a way as to ensure that we were both cooled by the breeze.
Her service was a punishment to me. My discomfiture at
having caved in to Ramcharan's insistence that I accept
his hospitality was increasing. I was responsible for this
and I felt the burden as no one else in the world had
ever felt it.

While Saraswati ate, Ramcharan prepared the baithak
outside for us. As soon as she arrived, he began declaiming
his poems. To cover my discomfort, I kept up a steady
stream of 'wah-wahs' as he read his love poetry. In order
to make sure Saraswati was getting as much of it as she
should, he would stop in between lines and I would
explain things to her. I was scared of her but I was also
trying to please her because I was so obligated to her.

It was very late when Ramcharan went inside,
completely happy. I do not know when my pain and
discomfiture subsided, for all at once, I fell asleep.

What woke me up was a sudden rain of blows, falling
at me from every direction. Ramcharan's room was full of
people. Among them were people who were abusing me,
accusing me of concealing my caste. There were others
who were cursing, reminding themselves of the proverb

that a snake in the house was asking to be butchered. And so they were doing their best to live up to the maxim. Ramcharan had gone from utmost devotion to demoniacal behaviour and was asking questions even as he hit me. He was enraged that his wife had served me and this was fuelling the fire of his anger which would not subside.

I gave up all hope of living. Sorrow and helplessness made my tongue heavy. Ramcharan's monstrous behaviour turned my insides to stone. And through it all, not a word came from my mouth, not a tear fell from my eyes. I fell where the blows took me. I took the punches as they came. I let the blood flow.

And Saraswati, who had no idea how to confront men, was shouting from the inside, 'Let him go. It's not his fault. He refused to come here. It was we who forced him to come. He has lost everything. Let him be or I'll throw myself over his body…'

As she was saying this, a commotion broke out outside. People began to run out. They were shouting to each other, 'Hey, that dheda gangster from Mumbai is attacking people with a knife. Run!'

Saraswati raced out into the baithak, lightning-swift, and whisked her husband in. She bolted the door and came and sat by my side and began to wipe the blood from my head and face with the pallu of her sari. Her eyes were exceptionally alert. Her gentle hands caressed my wounds, slowly lessening the shame I was feeling.

And then like a storm, Kashinath was in the room, knife flashing and shouting, 'Masthur, may you be blessed.'

His congratulations seemed like they might inflict

fresh wounds; and seeing him, Saraswati jumped to her feet and went to stand with her back to the door, ready to defend her husband.

'Out of my way,' shouted Kashinath, waving the knife at her. And so in order to protect her and make sure no harm came to her husband, I got to my feet, ignoring the pain in my body and said, 'Kashinath, let's go.'

He obeyed and as soon as he turned towards the baithak door, she raced, lightning-swift again, dropping the tears she had been holding back over my feet, and opened the inside door and went to Ramcharan. She was no longer afraid; and we could now leave the house.

Everything had been stolen from me. Ramcharan had ripped up my certificates and thrown them away. My head was bowed, my walk uncertain. My heart was a city rich with revolution. And Kashinath, with a naked knife in his hand, was roaring, ready to use it on all comers.

When we got out of the settlement, Kashinath said to me, 'Masthur, let's go to a police station.'

'No.'

'Why did you have to take those idiots' beating?'

'When was I beaten by them? It was Manu who thrashed me. Come, Kashinath…'

Translator's Acknowledgements

AS ALWAYS, MY gratitude to Shanta Gokhale and Neela Bhagwat.

And my thanks to all the Speaking Tigers, especially Radhika Shenoy for her meticulous editing.

BALUTA

Daya Pawar

Translated from the Marathi by Jerry Pinto

'[It has] taken three and a half decades for *Baluta*, the first Dalit autobiography in Marathi, to be made available in English...Jerry Pinto's translation makes the wait for *Baluta* worthwhile. This gut-wrenching, candid personal narrative, marked by linguistic variations, is sensitively interpreted for the contemporary English reader.'—*The Hindu*

'Daya Pawar's *Baluta* has enjoyed iconic status in Marathi literature...The hard-hitting portrayal of the life of an entire section of people from the Mahar caste, who for centuries had been treated as beasts of burden, as far less than human beings, had jolted upper-caste Marathi readers out of their self-complacency in the post-Independence euphoria...Unfortunately, *Baluta* had remained unavailable to English readers for a long time. Jerry Pinto's translation has filled that void.'—*The Indian Express*

'[An] outstanding example of self-writing...Pawar forcefully claims his place within contemporary Marathi literature as a passionate yet self-critical intellectual...Maharashtra has long been home to an indigenous radicalism that challenges caste hierarchies, and despite his reluctance to join a group such as the Dalit Panthers, Pawar ought to be seen as the heir to this radical intellectual tradition that harks back to Phule and Ambedkar.'—*Biblio*

I WANT TO DESTROY MYSELF: A MEMOIR

Malika Amar Shaikh

Translated from the Marathi by Jerry Pinto

'Malika Amar Shaikh's forthright self-portrait—and Jerry Pinto's translation that opens it to non-Marathi readers—is a disturbing yet luminous read.'—*Open*

'[Written] originally in Marathi, [Shaikh's memoir] kicked up a storm. It was not merely the memoir of a woman who had faced abuse at the hands of her husband Namdeo Dhasal, a revolutionary poet and a leading political figure. It also pointed to the contradictions within the Dalit movement in Maharashtra during the 1970s and the Dalit Panthers party that led it. Translated into English by Jerry Pinto as *I Want to Destroy Myself*, the book remains as powerful today, for Shaikh's is the story of a woman torn between the personal and the political, the Left and the Dalit movement, and her love and loathing for Dhasal.'—*The Indian Express*

'[A] searing tale of a promising young life blighted by an abysmal marriage…This translation from Marathi by Jerry Pinto is tender and unobtrusive. The image of "the girl with an unstoppable stream inside" and "a seven-storey laugh" is unforgettable.'—*Outlook*